I0575534

SUBURBAN JUNGLE & OTHER STORIES

JO AVENT

BRIZOPRESS

For Matt, Millie, and Sam

CONTENTS

SUBURBAN JUNGLE

ABBY, or Abigail Jones, as she had taken to introducing herself these days, licked her manicured thumb and wiped a smudge from her son, Matteo's, cheek. Luckily, she had noticed the unsightly smear before she sent him into the fray. She smoothed down his blonde hair, the same shade as her own, and, satisfied that he looked the part, helped him take a big step up into the big yellow school bus before climbing up behind him.

When the Joneses first moved into the tony neighborhood of Elmwood Park, their mortgage had been a stretch. Still, Abby had assured her husband that living there and having Matteo attend the prestigious Elmwood Park Elementary School wouldn't just give their only son the best start in life, it would open up opportunities for them all.

Abby was resourceful and a quick study; within just a few weeks, she leased the must-have German car, tracked down a second-hand version of this season's designer purse, and determined that, to break into the social scene, she had to become best friends with Julia Fairfax, President—Queen really—of the Parent Teacher Association.

Married to the owner of the hometown hockey team, Julia was the Godfather-esque ruler of Elmwood Park. Just like the Godfather, Julia had an entourage of lackeys that flocked around her and did her bidding. It seemed that no small part of Julia's bidding was keeping new people at arm's length. The rumor was that people close to Julia were invited to address her as Jools. Abby considered Abs for herself, but it didn't have the same ring.

Julia was a staple on the fundraising dinner circuit, had deep political and industry connections, and a place in Aspen. In short, the Joneses wanted to keep up with the Fairfaxes.

Ignoring the advice of an old friend who advised her that PTA stood for Parents To Avoid, she volunteered at an untold number of bake sales, raffles, and talent shows in hopes of starting a conversation with Julia, but was thwarted each time by her flunkeys.

Two weeks later, she got wind that Julia was chaperoning the third-grade trip to the local recycling plant. She had to snag one of the three other coveted spots. Knowing the sign-up slots would be released at 11.00 am, she refreshed the app every few seconds after 10.58 am. *Eras* tour tickets had been purchased with less determination. Her dedication paid off, and she made a mental note to teach Matteo about the importance of keeping a laser focus on one's goals.

On the bus, Matteo turned to his mother, "Mom," he started.

"Yes, sweetie," Abby said, looking over the top of his head, scanning the rows of seats for Julia—there she was sitting alone, a few rows back. Clad in black designer athleisure, she looked like a very wealthy burglar; toned pilates body—a jungle cat. Her chestnut hair cascaded from the baseball cap that hid her eyes, less a ponytail than the gleaming tresses of a thoroughbred.

"Mom," Matteo started again.

No time to talk. Abby dispatched Matteo further down the bus with a gentle shove. The only obstacle to sitting by Julia was Mr Reddy, the corduroy-vested science teacher. He was moving slowly up the aisle, checking the kids on his list. Seizing her opportunity to scoot past and misjudging the shrinking gap, she heard Mr Reddy's clipboard fall to the floor. No time to turn back—he probably had it under control.

Just as she was about to lower herself into position, she noticed a look of horror from two of Julia's lackeys, sitting in the row opposite. Of course, Julia would have the whole seat to herself. Correcting her faux pas, Abby sat down right in front of her target and extended an arm.

"Abigail Jones, pleased to meet you."

Julia was holding her phone in one hand and the "it" brand of insulated waterbottle in the other, which was also bedecked with a diamond ring the size of a quail's egg. She did not attempt to liberate either hand to shake Abby's.

Abby retracted her hand and felt Julia's discerning eye run over her, sizing her up. Like a submissive dog, she allowed herself to be inspected. During this metaphorical bottom sniffing, Abby was confident in the knowledge that she had nailed both her and Matteo's outfits.

Her son was wearing a scrupulously clean polo shirt with the correct small animal motif over his heart. It had taken some keen observation to select the right one, and she mused over the hierarchy. It seemed so arbitrary that a crocodile or a horse would trump a whale or a penguin. She, like Julia and her sidekicks, was dressed in merino wool, ready to commit a high-class breaking and entering. She fit right in; surely they would see that.

Julia gave her a polite nod, tiger's eyes meeting her gaze. "Julia Fairfax."

Abby sat. She was initially concerned that conversation would be difficult with Julia sitting directly behind her, but then realized it was perfect. Julia was trapped like a fly in a web, and Abby could control the interaction. She swiveled round to face her prey.

"My son is Matteo, who is your child?" she asked, an eager smile plastered across her face. She knew full well who Julia's son was—the third-grader with the most birthday invites. He was never dropped off by Julia herself, but always carpooled there by other moms, the ultimate power play.

"Sebastian," came the expected answer.

Abby had been coaching Matteo to make friends with the seven-year-old all year. She had engineered him onto the same Little League team, despite suspecting Matteo didn't enjoy baseball. She had been heartened to learn that Sebastian had recently borrowed his pencil sharpener. He had not given it back, but no matter! Abby was prepared to part with however much stationery it took to get closer to the Fairfaxes.

"Oh yes, Matty talks a lot about Sebastian. They seem to be developing quite a friendship!"

"He hasn't mentioned a Matteo," said Julia, botox preventing what would have no doubt been a brow furrowing on anyone else.

"We're new to the area this year," Abby continued, aware of the lackeys' eyes burning into her skin.

"Welcome," said Julia, her steady gaze not softening. "Where did you move from?"

"Downtown. Matteo was at the Grosvenor Montessori

for two years," said Abby. This was good. Grosvenor Montessori was unassailably high quality.

A flicker of recognition from Julia.

"Do you know the Marwood-Sinclairs?" she asked.

Abby froze. She racked her brain, but the name didn't ring a bell.

"Yes, lovely family," she said before she knew what she was doing.

"Didn't you say you were only there for a couple of years? They moved to North Carolina four years ago." Julia cocked her head to one side, but her expression remained inscrutable.

Abby flushed. Was it a trap? Savage if so. She mumbled something about confusing them with another family. She knew she didn't have long.

"It's wonderful that the PTA organizes these trips," she tried. "I'd love to work regularly with the organization. Are there any leadership roles coming up?"

Julia gestured to her henchwomen.

"You can get an application form to fill in. The team will review the applications over spring break." Julia's eyes slid toward the window.

"OK, thanks," Abby said. She was losing her. She needed a hook.

Abby faced forward for a moment before turning back to Julia for one last effort. She was big game hunting, and it was time to break out the big guns. There was one anecdote she had heard somewhere. She started chuckling as though she was revisiting a hilarious memory.

"I've got to tell you, it was so funny," she began. "In our previous school district, they canceled the fourth-grade trip to the Native American museum at the last minute."

Julia's frozen face showed a sliver of interest.

"It was scheduled the same day as Crazy Hair Day," Abby continued. "And half the boys had mohawks."

Julia was taking a sip of her drink. A lesser woman would have done a spit-take, but Julia just snorted a little and jerked her head.

A breakthrough! Abby sensed the feathers ruffling amongst the lackeys, just as she felt her own chest puffing out.

The windows on the bus rattled in place as the driver shifted into a lower gear to enter the parking lot. The passengers—Julia included—jerked forward a little in their seats as the full application of the brakes announced they had arrived at the recycling plant.

Abby exited the bus and stood in a group with Julia and the other moms while they waited for the kids to alight. She was thrilled that they were including her in the four. Abby was attentive to the conversation, conscious that her facial expressions were on point, mirroring the smiles and laughs of the other women, monkey see, monkey do, following in and joining in the conversation.

During a pause, Julia turned to her. "Abigail, this weekend, we're having a small baseball party. Perhaps you and your family would like to join?"

Before she could answer, one of the lackeys tapped Abby on the arm and pointed. "Abigail, isn't that your son?"

It took Abby a moment to transition from the dopamine hit of being invited to the Fairfaxes and process the scene. Matteo was in the middle of a throng of kids. He looked upset. Her body set off toward him before it was a conscious choice. He was in tears, his little face flushed, his button nose snotty. With a pang of distress, she saw that a tall-for-his-age boy was jeering at him. Sebastian. She had never disliked a child more.

On approach, she heard the tall boy say, "Soccer's for little kids! No one cares about running up and down a field. Zero-zero - woohoo!"

"Shut up, Sebastian," said a bespectacled girl with two auburn pigtails. "People should do what they enjoy!"

"Be quiet, Daphne," Sebastian retorted. "No one cares what you think."

"I care what you think, Daphne!" said Abby, scooping Matteo into her arms. She carried him to the quiet side of the bus before setting him down and crouching to his level.

"Mom," he said, his voice quiet, lower lip trembling, and breathing ragged. His blue eyes were watery through his long, wet lashes.

Something in Abby cracked.

"What, honey?" she asked, smoothing down a blond tuft, now damp along the hairline.

"I tried to tell you I don't like baseball," he managed to get out between sobs. "The kids are mean, and I'm not good at it. I like soccer."

"Then we'll switch to soccer," she said. It was an easy decision.

"No more Little League?"

"No," she said.

"I'm not in trouble?" he asked, body still shaking.

"Of course not!" she said, hugging him to her. And then she remembered what the little girl had said. "People should do what they enjoy."

When Matteo had calmed down, Abby took his hand and they regrouped with the rest of the party.

"Jools," Abby felt she had earned that one. "Thank you for the invite, but we won't be able to come to the baseball party this weekend."

She stood with the Moms in the group, but her mind was

elsewhere. That Daphne girl had seemed nice. She resolved to research her parents when she got home. Perhaps it would be worth orchestrating a playdate with her?

A PIECE OF MEAT

ALICE WALKED around her Brooklyn apartment, putting away the last items of mismatched crockery from the drying rack. She watered her plants, dangling in macramé slings, and topped up the water in Mitzy's bowl. Although money was tight, she had a good eye for thrift store finds. Her one-bedroom place was frayed around the edges but still homely and comfortable.

She counted the change in her coin purse and grabbed a couple of cloth bags. In the dark hallway, she tidied her messy blond bangs in the small mirror. Then, she affectionately ruffled Mitzy's fur, smoothing her hands over the dog's muzzle and ears.

"I won't be gone long. Just popping to the store for supplies."

Mitzy cocked her head to one side, all puppy dog eyes.

"Ah, sweet girl, I know, I'll miss you too. Maybe I'll pick up a treat for you," Alice said.

Her heavy door had two chunky locks, a chain, and a deadbolt. In the hallway, while she locked up behind her, she was confronted with the chaos of other people. A strong smell hit her: Fabuloso, the purple cleaning fluid favored by her neighbors. She didn't mind the scent, but thought labeling it lavender was false advertising. A blaring TV, an angry mom, a schoolkid practicing the trumpet, a baby crying. She picked her way past mismatched doormats, a stroller, a bag of recycling, and various pairs of footwear before making it out onto the street.

Women living alone in the city can't be too careful, she'd been warned when she moved to New York. At first, she had found all the safety measures limiting. No walking alone at night, but if you are walking alone at night, choose a busy, well-lit route, and hold your keys between your fingers. Don't get out of the taxi in front of your house; otherwise, they'll know where you live. Get a dog, you'll feel safer. Sweet Mitzy was no guard dog. She never even barked when a stranger came in. This thought made her smile.

She wasn't single by choice; being on her own was a tough experience. She'd love to meet someone special, but to say that dating in the city had been hard would be a vast understatement—a carousel of cads looking for an easy lay.

It would be nice to have someone to share things with and to feel safe with. It would be nice to meet someone authentic who liked her for her. Someone who took the time to speak to her. She yearned for an actual partner to do life with. It was so hard to know who to trust, though. Letting someone in meant taking a risk.

The first time a passing car honked at her, she was twelve years old, in her school uniform. Alice was 'a pretty young thing'. She took that feedback to heart and tried to make herself smaller than she already was. That meant no make-up, no tight clothes, no bright colors. She hated the way they looked at her as if she were prey. She didn't want them to notice her. She didn't want to deal with what came next.

Her stomach lurched at an unpleasant, more recent memory of an unfortunate encounter that made her change her routine. She made sure to vary her route after that and not shop in the same store too frequently. The guy had been friendly at first, and she had been so hopeful. But then he insisted on coming back to her house. She had tried to say no. She had felt so much shame as she cleaned up the mess he had made. What was his name? Steve? Simon?

A passerby catcalled her at the bus stop. She put the hood up on her hoodie, only lowering it again when she arrived at her destination, a bodega six blocks from her home. She had only been there a couple of times, but having been followed before, she liked to keep her routine unpredictable. It didn't feel safe when people knew her movements.

The bell tinkled above the bodega door as she opened it and stepped inside. The air was thick and musty. An incense stick on the counter was out-gunned by stale coffee, overripe fruit, and a miscellaneous fried smell from the hot food counter. She didn't prefer this store; it was on the larger side, and the layout was labyrinthine. Alice tucked a wire shopping basket into the crook of her left arm. She wrinkled her nose and considered that the smell without the incense stick might be worse.

Aside from a disinterested older woman who didn't look up and was barely visible behind a colorful display of chewing gum, the store was empty.

Alice made her way through the aisles. To her, each bodega was like a museum where you could touch the exhibits. She stood by the spice section for a long time, taking in the different jars and faded boxes with exotic-sounding names. She imagined the extravagant dishes she could make with the unfamiliar ingredients.

At the end of the aisle, she was delighted to find a fat

tabby cat, lying on its side, napping on a stack of cereal boxes. New York bodegas were famous for having cats, which she supposed was to deter rats. She reached out to smooth the sleeping animal. It luxuriated under her touch and stretched out its front and back legs, as though leaping through the air, not bothering to open its eyes. Ah, the luxury of being safe in your space and knowing nothing bad could happen to you.

"He likes that." A man's voice startled her. She pulled her hand back and turned to see a tall man with dark hair about her age. He was smiling. And then, "Sorry, didn't mean to make you jump."

Alice sized him up. He was handsome. Maybe he didn't mean to scare her, but his amused face sure suggested he was enjoying that he had. Or was he just being friendly? Was this going to be another Steve? Or Simon? Whatever his name was. She hoped not, but she couldn't be sure.

She had learned the hard way, through years of experience, that it was best to play along—act as though there had been no ill intent, so as not to provoke so she could get away safely. No one was more dangerous than a Nice Guy who suspected you thought he wasn't a Nice Guy.

"No problem," she said with forced, but plausible brightness. What an actress!

There was a moment of awkward silence until she backed away, tucking herself around the corner by the baking ingredients. From there, she could see in the round mirror, mounted to monitor shoplifters, that he was following her. She picked up a bag of flour and pretended to study it, flicking her glance to the mirror to keep an eye on him, waiting to see what he would do next.

"Making a cake?" he asked.

"Oh, no," she said. "Well, maybe. It's always a bit sad to make a cake for one, though, isn't it?"

Had she said too much? The eyebrow raise was almost imperceptible, but she spotted it. A girl alone in the city has to notice things like that.

"You live alone?" He licked his lips.

"Yeah, just me and Mitzy, my dog," she put the flour back on the shelf.

"I do too, just moved here." He put out his hand to shake hers, "Griff, pleased to meet you."

"Alice," she said. She wasn't sure how she felt about meeting him yet.

"OK, well, I don't want to get in your way," he said and took a step back.

She smiled at him. Perhaps he was different. She gave a little shrug and moved over to the meat section.

She picked up a piece of steak. It looked crimson, bulging, and obscene under plastic wrap. She wondered what marbling was. She knew marbling was good, but wasn't sure how to spot it. She picked up another piece of meat.

He was next to her again.

Her heartbeat sped up.

"Steak, huh?" he said.

"Er, yeah, maybe," she said. "Do you know about marbling?"

A small test, of course. Would he condescend to her? Mansplain?

"Enough to know you're not going to get a great marbled steak at a bodega," he said. That smile again, his teeth were straight and white. She felt her cheeks warm. "This one has a huge piece of fat that you'll end up throwing away. This pack's your best bet. Two pieces in here, you can eat one and freeze one."

"Thanks," she said, putting the pack he suggested in her basket.

He mimed a salute as she slid past him to pay for her groceries.

Outside on the street, he caught up with her again.

"Hey, Alice! Check out what I picked up. Your steak would go nicely with this stuff. " He opened his shopping bag to show her and flashed another smile. He had a bottle of red wine, some potatoes, and broccoli.

"Huh. Yeah, it would," she said.

"Look, I never normally do this," he said. "But how about we put all this together to make a decent meal and eat it together?"

She bit her lip. This was too fast. There was something about him, though. Maybe this time would be different.

"We both get a steak dinner for half the price! You can come over to mine, I'll cook for us both!" he said.

She appraised him again. He was big, plump, almost. He was quick to smile. Was it real? It was sweet that he wanted to cook for her. That was a green flag, right? Everyone knew the first rule of dating was that you don't go to the guy's place on the first meeting. She mentally totted up the risks and rewards of his proposition. She was intrigued, and sometimes you have to take a chance to meet someone.

"Why don't you come to my place?" she said finally.

They agreed he would come over at 7.00 pm that evening. She gave him her address on a piece of paper.

Alice second-guessed her decision on the bus ride home from the bodega. She was usually more careful. It had been ages since she had done this, and the last time didn't go well. Steve, that was his name. She usually waited until she knew them better so she could be sure. Had anyone even seen them together at the bodega? Would anyone even know if something happened?

At 6:50 pm, Alice was still getting ready. She chose a

blue dress she had owned for a while. It was flattering without making her feel like she was on show. She still needed to work out this guy's deal.

At 7:00 pm on the dot, her doorbell rang. There was an awkward moment as she thought he was going for a peck on the cheek, and he hugged her. She brushed it off, no big deal. He, too, had changed for dinner; he was now wearing a linen short-sleeved shirt and slacks. They moved into the kitchen. He, rather hurriedly, she felt, opened the wine and poured them both a glass. She noticed he had brought two bottles with him.

They set about preparing the food. He took her largest knife and made short work of the vegetables. Piles of neat cubes of potato and little green trees of broccoli grew on the chopping board. Alice found the sight of his big hand gripping the knife handle—his forearm rippled with muscle—both appealing and unnerving.

The steak sizzled in a cast-iron skillet, and the smell of cooked meat filled the air. They'd agreed on medium rare. They laughed together as she cut the steak into strips, red juice spilling freely onto the chopping board, pooling around the rim. Alice started to think perhaps this one was different.

Over dinner, they reminisced about their childhood, their first jobs, and their current jobs. They talked about travels, where they had been, and where they would like to go. He kept topping up her glass. Her numb cheeks and fuzzy head told her she'd had enough. A few times she'd told him not to top up her glass, but he had done it anyway. That was confusing. She hoped so much he wouldn't turn out to be just like the last one.

After dinner, she got up to clear the plates away. He got up too and asked her about dessert. Her head was spinning, or the room was. She hadn't thought about dessert. She apologized.

"I think you're the dessert, babe, " he told her, his pupils large with desire, darkening his whole face. He bit his lower lip. She hadn't noticed his large incisors before.

She took a step back until she felt the sink against the small of her back. It felt good to have something steadying behind her, but it meant she was unable to retreat further. He took a step toward her. He was much taller than her. Her breath came ragged in her throat. Keep it light, she told herself.

"Wouldn't you prefer some ice cream?" she said in what she hoped was a joking tone.

"No, babe," he said, taking another step closer. Her unfocused gaze found his again. His eyes were locked on her. "I think I'd rather have you."

"It's chocolate brownie flavor!" she continued. She wanted it not to be true, for him to stop the escalation. She didn't want what would inevitably come next.

"Don't come any closer," she mustered up her most serious voice. It was impossible to play this off as a misunderstanding now.

"You don't mean that," he said, undeterred.

"I don't want this," firmer now. "Stay back."

"Oh, come on, you knew what was going to happen."

Her mind was foggy, but the similarities to the last one were undeniable now. Here we go again. He moved to grab her wrist, but this time she didn't move away. Her fear had evaporated, replaced by calm resignation. She had the luxury of being safe in her space and knowing nothing bad could happen to her.

"Mitzy," she called. "I got you a treat."

Griff took a beat to consider this change in her demeanor.

A low growl emanated from the bedroom doorway. He turned to see a huge beast, the biggest dog he had ever seen. With a thick, shaggy coat of grey and white fur, it looked like a wolf slowly rounding the corner. Griff kept hold of Alice's wrist, but his grip loosened.

"What the...?" he said.

"This is Mitzy. I told you about her!" Alice sounded a lot more relaxed now.

Mitzy snarled, yellow eyes fixed on Griff, her black lips retracted to reveal teeth like daggers.

Griff dropped Alice's wrist to put both hands up in front of him.

"Good dog," he said, trying to sound light, making himself smaller.

The animal lowered herself to a crouch, snarling, saliva dripping from her mouth.

"Alice, get her to relax," Griff pleaded. He sounded desperate.

"It didn't have to be this way," said Alice with a sigh.

Mitzy slunk closer to Griff, huge paw after huge paw, padding closer to him. Her intent was clear.

"Call off your fucking dog!" Griff yelled, his desperation escalating to anger directed at Alice.

That was the trigger. Mitzy hunched lower before springing across the room in a sleek arc of raw power. Griff's raised hands were no match for the weight and strength of the animal. She sank her teeth into his shoulder where it tore through his neck, bringing him down onto the kitchen floor. Poor Griff tried vainly to struggle, but it was all over in a matter of moments.

"Good girl, Mitzy," Alice said. So many people had given her safety tips when she moved to the city, and those people were right. She did feel safer having a dog.

After Mitzy was done with her treat, Alice sighed. This was the worst part: cleaning up. She surveyed the mess. Steve made much less of a mess than this new guy. What was his name again? Greg? Craig? It hardly mattered.

Mitzy gnawed on a femur as Alice set about mopping up the blood. "You just don't know who you can trust these days."

Stopping for a break. She put her hands and chin on the end of the mop. "Mitzy, I wonder if this would all be simpler if you would just bark when they get here, so they know you're here," she mused. "Then maybe they'd behave themselves?"

METAMORPHOSIS

IN A TREEHOUSE, Parker stood up, modeling her new sneakers. She twirled this way and that so that the glitter on the laces caught the light just right.

"Awesome, Parker!" the Johnson twins, Josie and Jilly, cooed in unison, with just a slight lisp caused by their new braces. "So cool!"

The seating arrangements in the treehouse were basic. The twins sat cross-legged on an old Persian rug commandeered from a pile destined for the goodwill store. The only chair, a low-slung beach chair, remained unoccupied since Bridget stopped hanging out with them.

Parker allowed herself a small smile. The shoes were a rare new item for her, as she was more accustomed to hand-me-downs from her older siblings. And here she was, basking in Bridget's old limelight. Time for a new queen? It was delicious.

Clunking sounds from the rope ladder interrupted the fashion show.

"Halt! Who's there?" said Parker.

"It's me, Bridget."

The treehouse trio was wide-eyed. Bridget!

"What do we do?" panicked Josie.

"Can she come in?" asked Jilly.

"Wait there!" Parker ordered. Turning to the Johnsons, she added, "She hasn't exactly been a great friend lately."

The twins nodded, and their shoulders drooped.

Parker felt warm inside at their deference to her.

It had been a few days since Bridget had stopped making bracelets with them at lunchtime. The first day she was absent, they kept expecting her to show up, but after repeated sightings of her walking away, blond curls bouncing in her hot pink scrunchie, arm in arm with her new BFFs, they began to accept the foursome had become a three.

"Can she earn her way back in?" suggested Jilly.

A fat caterpillar inching along a twig caught Parker's attention. She picked it up between her thumb and forefinger.

"Tell her to come up," she said.

Bridget joined the girls in the small space.

"What did I miss?" she asked.

"Well, we've been making shrinky dinks and—" Josie started.

"You can't just walk back in here and be our friend again," interrupted Parker, hand on her hip.

"Fine. What do you want me to do?" asked Bridget, matching the hand on hip stance.

"Kiss the caterpillar," Parker said. She thrust the creepy crawly out until it was a couple of inches in front of Bridget's nose.

Bridget barely hesitated. She kissed the writhing green creature.

The twins cheered, delighted at the promise of reunion.

Parker felt a rush go through her. But this was a delicious new thrill; the electricity of supremacy.

"That was too easy for you. If you're truly sorry, you'll eat the caterpillar." She said.

Gasps all around.

"It's too much, Parker!" said the twins.

Parker felt giddy.

"That's the price," she said.

Bridget locked Parker in a steely gaze. She popped the caterpillar into her mouth. Her hand dropped from its place on her hip, and her fists balled. Her eyes watered a little as she chewed. Finally, with a scrunched face and a big gulp, the creature was gone.

The twins' expressions shifted from horror to hope. They turned to Parker, the question was written across their eager faces, awaiting the verdict.

A week ago, Parker would have looked to Bridget that way, in search of answers, seeking a cue. But a week is a long time in middle school. Parker, Nero of the treehouse, with Bridget's fate in her hands, gave a single nod. She could afford to be magnanimous.

The twins cheered.

With a sigh of relief, Bridget moved toward the low-slung beach chair to reprise her throne. A glittery sneaker-clad foot stepped in her way.

"You're there," said Parker, pointing to a spot on the rug between the twins, who scooted over to make room for her.

No one in the treehouse breathed.

After the tiniest moment of hesitation, Bridget took her place between the twins.

Parker lowered herself onto the chair with a reverence fitting a coronation, which of course it was.

Things looked different from her elevated position. She liked it a lot.

HOLIDAY MAGIC

TONY NARROWED his eyes at the box of holiday lights as though sizing up an opponent. A tangle of twisted wires punctuated by red, green, and gold bulbs taunted him. It had been a long day of meetings in the Notting Hill design agency, but with an important client visiting the next day, he needed to get the decorations up before leaving. He let out a long sigh.

The building, a repurposed Victorian family home, was quiet at this time of day. Through the sash window, the first flakes of the season swirled outside.

"Anything I can help with?"

Tony looked up to see Seth from marketing, leaning on the doorframe, backpack slung over his shoulder, eyebrow raised, with an amused grin on his face. He'd noticed that cheeky smile before and had even been brave enough to return it once or twice.

"Aren't you headed home?" Tony didn't want to be a bother.

"I was about to lock up, but I like a challenge!"

Tony set the box down on the wooden floor. Seth rolled

up his sleeves. As they got to work untangling the lights, their hands brushed against each other. Tony made no attempt to avoid these mini collisions. Was he imagining it, or was Seth not avoiding them either?

They had exchanged glances—that Tony found hard to decipher—over the tops of their monitors or passing on the stairs, but this was only the second time they had been alone together.

Tony had been making tea in the kitchen for the first time. He had fallen into the trap of offering it to everyone. Seth walked in to find him with a dozen or so mismatched mugs of tea lined up on the countertop.

"Right, I've got 'World's Best Dad', the dinosaur one, and '#1 Boss'," said Seth. "You grab the Manchester United one, the cat one, and 'This Might Be Wine'. We'll come back for the rest."

After they had distributed the tea, their paths hadn't crossed again until tonight.

"Why are holiday lights always tangled?"

"Ah, that's the magic of the season!" said Seth, his dark curls springing as he wrestled with a knot. "The lights will be even more spectacular because we worked for them."

"Thanks for helping. I would have been here until midnight."

"Yeah, well, no point rushing home to an empty flat," said Seth.

"You live alone?" asked Tony.

"Since my ex moved out in March."

"Oh." Tony was surprised by how squeaky his voice sounded. He added, changing the subject, "How's your gift shopping going?"

"Nearly everyone taken care of," said Seth. "Just need something for Dad. I want to get him something really special. It's been a difficult year—we lost Mum over the summer."

"Oh, I'm so sorry," said Tony, putting down the lights. "I lost my Dad last year."

A wave of understanding passed between them. Tony felt, and suppressed, a strong urge to reach out to Seth and take him in his arms. Instead, he took a deep breath and resumed untangling.

At last, with all the strands liberated, Seth hopped up onto a desk and then onto a filing cabinet. "Pass them up?"

Tony did as he was asked, but it looked dangerous, and he couldn't help but add, "Be careful up there."

Seth parkoured his way across the office furniture, looping the strand over artwork, weaving it through a ficus plant, and stretching to pin it into the cornices while a nervous Tony looked on.

At last, it was time. Seth hopped down, and Tony, with a cry of "Et voilà!" put the plug in the socket.

The room came alive with radiant color. Their eyes met, and Tony thought he felt a flicker of meaning pass between them. He wondered if this was the moment to make a move when, without warning, every monitor and lamp cut out, plunging them into darkness.

"Did I just kill Christmas?" groaned Tony.

"Ha! No, just the circuit breaker tripped," said Seth, feeling for the wall. "Happened in my old flat whenever anyone tried to use the toaster and the kettle at the same time."

"Must have made breakfast interesting!"

"You have no idea," Seth chuckled.

They headed to the breaker box in the hallway, by the light of Tony's cellphone. Tony caught an edge of Seth's cologne—sandalwood and amber—as they stood there together. Feeling Seth's warmth so close in the dark, he wanted to fall into it, but held himself back. Had he imagined their moment earlier? He needed to be sure.

At the box, Seth flipped a switch with practiced ease, restoring light to the building and filling the room with twinkling color up the walls and ceiling again. He leaned against a stationery cupboard, admiring their handiwork. Tony moved next to him, but kept a distance of a few inches from Seth. The pull was so strong, but he didn't quite dare act. Not yet.

"We're a good team," smiled Seth.

"We are," said Tony. "And you were right about the lights, they are even more spectacular."

They stood in silence. Tony felt—not quite nervous—no, that wasn't it. It was the weight of a moment when it was imbued with possibility. He took a chance.

"You know, the shops will still be open on Kensington High Street," he said. "If you would like, we could go shopping for something for your Dad."

Seth turned toward him.

"I'd really like that."

Tony moved closer to him, his body weight gently, but unmistakably, leaning into the other man.

Seth took his hand.

It was magical, Tony thought; the knowing.

THE BRIDGE

EARLIER THIS SPRING, I learned Cara Thompson had been paroled and was headed here, to The Bridge. Of course, I've always understood this might happen someday, that the woman incarcerated twenty years ago for my sister Amy's murder would show up here. And it is unnerving that she'll be close, but part of me feels safer keeping tabs on her. Like seeing a spider in your bedroom, it's somehow worse when you can't see it anymore.

The Bridge is a big, red brick building that could have been an orphanage a hundred years ago. It now houses a couple of dozen women transitioning from the maximum security state prison back to normal life. The forecourt is tarmacked, with no plants to beautify the space, a deliberate design decision to avoid encouraging the homeless folks who gather anyway. The Program Director worries they're dealing drugs. Some of them are.

Since Amy's death, I don't need to work, so for the past few years, I've spent a couple of days a week coaching residents on their résumés and offering interview tips. I know something about turning your life around and rebuilding yourself.

Opulence has no place at The Bridge, and I don't want to stick out. My silk blouses and cashmere sweaters don't belong here. I'm wearing my volunteer uniform. It's a thrift-store dress, one of a few on rotation, bought for this purpose. It's a cornflower shade that accentuates my blue eyes and my, now, auburn hair.

I am waiting in my office for her to arrive. Will she recognize me? I take a sip of stale coffee and a deep breath. I thumb through the pages of her case file. Some of it is familiar, details about the period after her sentencing, when she spent a few years protesting her innocence—a very stressful time for me.

They never found the murder weapon, a fact she used as part of her defence, but they had enough without it. It was a small kitchen knife. I know the one. It has an orange handle and was dropped at some point, so the tip is slightly bent.

After her appeal, it appears Cara settled well into prison life. She was a model prisoner in fact.

She and Amy met as Amy's consulting business was taking off, and they soon started dating. It was the first time Amy had brought another woman home, and I wondered if Mom and Dad would disapprove of this new move by perfect Amy, but they didn't mind at all. My elder sister could do no wrong.

By the time they were married, Amy owned a house in the nice part of downtown and a couple of rental properties. Aside from the wedding, I only met Cara a handful of times. Amy and I weren't close in those days.

The door opens slowly, and there she is. She is shorter than I remember; she appears cowed. Her olive skin looks pale, or perhaps that's the institutional grey paint on the walls. The way she holds her body, she is lupine. It could get dangerous for me if she recognizes me.

She takes a seat. I release the breath I'd been holding in and introduce myself. For once, I am grateful to the loser I married and divorced in my early twenties for giving me a different surname from Amy. I give Cara the usual spiel, outlining the job application processes and how to handle questions about her crime and incarceration.

It's only at the end, as I hand her the particulars for her next day's interviews, that she looks me in the eyes for the first time.

"Where did you say you were from again?" She asks.

"Local to here," I say.

"Right. You look a bit like someone I used to know," she cocks her head on one side.

"Oh, I get that a lot," I laugh and try to sound breezy.

Something in her face shifts. Recognition?

"Shit," I say under my breath as the door closes behind her.

Overnight, I can't sleep, obsessing over the thought that Cara is close. That she recognized me. That she is coming for me.

The next morning, I arise late and make tea. Technically, it's Amy and Cara's old house, but I've been here so long I don't think of it like that now. I don't even think of Amy's body in the living room anymore.

I take my tea, dunking the tea bag in and out, enjoying the honey ginger aroma, and stand by the French window. I love this park view. I wonder how Cara is doing at her interviews.

As though that thought summoned her, there she is, out in the street, looking this way. I jump back, and hot tea spills on my hand. Did she see me? Panic rises in my chest. I move to the corner of the window, so as not to be seen from the outside, and peek out. There's no mistaking it's Cara.

What's she planning?

At my next shift at The Bridge, I waste no time. Volunteers aren't allowed into the bedrooms, but with everyone in the common areas, I sneak upstairs. Cara is assigned to bedroom three. My senses heighten, amidst the mismatched, donated furniture, I race to look through her things. Photos of her and Amy smiling, on vacation, at a picnic, I flip past those, looking for anything that relates to me.

A wedding photo. It's blurry, but there I am, dyed black hair, hollow cheeks, thirty pounds lighter, barely making it through the ceremony without needing to go and shoot up. I've come so far since those days—with the help of Amy's assets.

Looking at the wedding photo, I'm back there. It was a picture-perfect outdoor affair at our parents' house, white roses and a blue-sky California day. I know Mom and Dad advised Amy against inviting me. They had cut me off long ago, but she had insisted and wouldn't hear otherwise.

Amy could be headstrong once she had made up her mind. She asked me to be part of her bridal party. At the reception, she gave me a pearl necklace on a gold chain as a bridesmaid gift. I told her I'd rather have had the cash.

My being in the wedding party was against Cara's wishes too; she hadn't liked me at first sight. At the rehearsal dinner, I was going through coat pockets in the entryway closet, looking for spare change, and I heard them arguing about it out on the porch. Cara accused Amy of enabling me, which she denied, of course. But it was true. She was my oasis for anything I needed. She was my safety net, and the only thing keeping me off rock bottom—until I turned up at her work that time. She drew a line there, saying it was the last straw.

When she cut me off, I had to crawl my way back from a very dark hole. She never knew how much that decision changed everything for me.

Footsteps on the stairs make me freeze. Blood is rushing in my ears, and I struggle to hear. Someone is coming. Adrenaline jolts me into action. I slide the photo up my shirt and replace it with something else. The footsteps stop, and there's conversation on the landing. It is Cara. She's so close to me, she must hear me, *smell* me. A voice downstairs calls her name, and I hear the footsteps fading. While the coast is clear, I slip out of her room.

A couple of evenings later, I'm making dinner, a chicken and bacon recipe I've been wanting to try, when I get the email that Cara failed the conditions of her parole. Contraband was found during a routine search, as I knew it would be. The photo is safe with me, and there's nothing to link me to Cara. Relief washes through me like it's purifying me. My secret is so much safer with her back in prison. I pour myself a glass of wine. Since NA, I rarely indulge, but I'm celebrating tonight, a job well done.

It is handy having the homeless folks just outside The Bridge. I wouldn't know where to buy smack these days without them.

I chop the bacon. Even though the tip is bent, the little orange-handled knife still works well. I'll work a few more shifts at The Bridge and then give in my notice. There's nothing more for me there now.

WHERE ANGELS FEAR TO TREAD

THE TOAD WAS the latest gift left on our doorstep by our benevolent cat. Belly up and arms outstretched as though crucified. He looked so pitiful, I buried him, decorating the mound with daisies, dandelion heads, and small pebbles.

Fools rush in, as they say. I wasn't a fool exactly—I was eight, just a kid.

The next day, I found the pile of earth erupted, flowers in disarray, stones rolled away, and no toad. Hot guilt rushed to my cheeks. I hadn't checked for a pulse. He seemed dead.

I decided he wasn't buried alive; this was a miracle.

THE RESCUE

PULLING into the stop on Chicago's Michigan Avenue, the bus brakes screech. Josh quits his game and slides his phone into his pocket. He only lives about a mile from his work, but rain or shine, he prefers to take the bus so he can play or scroll through the news; it doesn't matter which.

As he moves down the aisle to exit, he stops to allow a young woman to get out of her row.

"What a gentleman," she says, smiling, twisting her dark curly hair around her fingers, stepping out in front of him. As the line shuffles forward, she turns back a couple of times to smile at him.

She's attractive, but she's acting so strangely, slowing them down. Josh tries to be patient and gives her a tight-lipped smile in an attempt to speed things up. Waiting for the doors to open, he grips the rail with his left hand and realizes the woman is inspecting it. It's a perfectly normal hand. Self-conscious, he slides it out of sight into his pocket, switching to his right hand.

He catches his reflection in the bus window. He tucks his white shirt into his slate-grey pants and straightens his light jacket. He frowns a little at the salt and pepper around his temples. At thirty-two, he thinks he is a bit young to be going grey, but then remembers his parents were married with children by his age. He's too young for all that; much better this way.

Sure, there had been girlfriends before, one was even serious, but after an escalation of miscommunications and a mountain of mutual resentments, she left. In the early days after her departure, he had felt an almost intolerable ache. The ache was less when he played his games or perused the forums. It eventually subsided.

The hydraulic doors hiss open, allowing Josh and about twenty others to scatter off the bus. Downtown is home to showstopping skyscrapers that halt tourists in their tracks. They plant on the sidewalk to marvel, craning their necks, which irritates Josh as he has to step around them.

A block before he arrives at his building, he gets coffee. He joins the long line of office workers dressed in conservative shades and scrolls through social postings on his phone. He orders the same thing, a flat white, from the same auburn goateed barista every day. Josh has his earbuds in, as always, so aside from putting in his order, they have never exchanged a word.

In the elevator on the way up to his office, a TV is playing on a loop. It shows news headlines and commercials. Everyone in the elevator faces the screen, as though plugged in by the eyeballs, released only when the doors open to their floor and they head to their desk.

On the forty-seventh floor, Josh gets out. The windows in the office have the blinds lowered to prevent glare on their computer screens. In his cubicle, he pores over spreadsheets, analyzes data, and meets targets. Josh's mom tells her friends he does "something in finance."

At 11 a.m., Josh heads to the kitchen area. It's Bagel Thursday, an initiative by Gabi from HR to boost community in the office. It doesn't work. Everyone takes their baked treat back to their desk to eat. Today, lots of people are working from home, and tons of bagels are left over.

"Might as well take two," says Gabi, leaning on the kitchen island, head propped up on an elbow, her long dark hair scraping the countertop.

"If you say so," says Josh with a shrug, piling another onto his plate.

Even though it is still light outside, his apartment is in darkness when he returns home, due to his habit—developed the previous winter—of not opening his blinds. Pointless to open them every morning to come home in the dark and just have to close them again every evening anyway. Now he turns on the lights and rips the cellophane off a microwave dinner, which, once heated, he can't finish. He thinks to himself that he must have had a big lunch, but he can't remember what it had been.

After dinner, it's Josh's routine to play online computer games with old college friends who live in other big cities. One of his friends recently dropped out of the group after a romantic relationship had turned serious. He hopes none of the rest of the group meets anyone, and then he feels bad. He wonders, feeling the familiar ache starting to rise inside him again, how, or if, he will meet someone.

He grabs his phone and swipes through the comforting, colorful squares on his homescreen. He refreshes his email, nothing urgent. The ache, though still there, stops growing. There were always the dating apps, he supposed. Finding no new texts, he shoots off a reply to a message from his mom from yesterday. The ache soothes a little. Plenty of time for the apps and getting back out there when he felt ready again.

After a couple of minutes scrolling through the Chicago Bears subreddit, the ache subsides entirely.

Before logging on to the game, he puts his unfinished dinner in the trash and takes the full trash bag outside to the bins.

He is lowering the garbage can lid when a movement in the corner of his eye catches his attention. Braced to fend off a raccoon—he'd heard stories —he is relieved to see a medium-sized dog about twenty feet from him, tucked behind a garage.

The dog shrinks itself under Josh's gaze, but stays where it is.

"What's up, buddy? You get out of your yard?"

The dog steps forward, sniffing the air. Josh estimates the animal is about forty pounds. Its dull, dark coat is matted into thick cords of fur, and it has no collar. Its ears are folded over, and its tail is erect in a big plume—a stray.

"Ah, you're hungry. Well, come on over, I've got just the thing."

Josh opens the bin back up and undoes the tie on the garbage he just deposited to retrieve his unfinished dinner. He sets it down about ten feet from the dog.

"There you go, friend. Beef lasagne."

The dog eyes the food hungrily, but doesn't move. Josh steps back. The dog looks at the food and looks at Josh. Its twinkly eyes in a furry face, more teddy bear than wolf, interrogate him.

"It's OK," he says. "It's not the type with vegetables in it."

The dog cocks its head to one side as though considering the statement and sniffs its way toward the food.

"Sorry, it's not much."

The dog gulps down the food in three bites, licks the container, and then sets about eating that too.

Josh wonders if he should remove the tray, but doesn't want to risk a bite and thinks it's probably OK; the cardboard will help to fill it up. The dog looks at him and lets out a small whimper, and Josh reads its expression clearly: it wants more food.

"OK, wait here."

He goes back up to his apartment and heats another one of his microwave meals.

"Meatloaf," he says, placing the meal on the ground and crouching to make himself less intimidating.

The dog eats the second meal with equal gusto, pausing every few bites to look at Josh with a softness in its eyes.

Josh, sitting cross-legged on the ground, perceives gratitude in the eye contact. It has been a long time since he's been looked at that way. He sits up a little straighter.

"Good pup."

When the dog finishes the meal and most of the packaging, it studies Josh before dropping and rolling over onto its back.

"You want pets, good boy?" says Josh. He approaches the animal with care, weighing his next move. The dog doesn't look rabid; stray dogs can be unpredictable, but this one appears friendly. On the other hand, there's a decent likelihood the dog has fleas, and no doubt he's dirty. Seeming to sense Josh's dilemma, the dog ups the ante and starts wagging its tail. Finding the invitation irresistible, Josh offers up his hand for smelling before stroking the dog under his chin. He has read somewhere that it is good for their self-esteem.

"How did you enjoy your dinner?" he asks.

The tail wagging intensifies. Josh guesses the dog's

heritage: a bit of lab with that temperament, terrier for the flopped-over button ears, and maybe some doodle for the fur.

"Oh. Good," Josh moves to rubbing the dog's belly in big circles, feeling some stress he didn't realize he was carrying melt away. "And did you prefer the lasagne or the meatloaf?"

Josh pauses to allow an answer.

"Me too, bud. You know, I think this is the longest conversation I've had all day."

The truth of this thought spoken out loud sends a pang through Josh's chest. Could that be right? Josh cups the dog's ears, scratching and rubbing them. He snaps a photo of the dog, and then, on a whim, takes a selfie of them both together.

"Certainly the best conversation I've had all day."

The two sit together in the warm evening air for a while before the clattering of a garbage can lid two doors down breaks the spell. In an instant, the startled dog is on its feet and gone, down the alley.

Josh waves in resignation, getting to his feet.

"You're welcome for the food," he calls after the dog, turning to go back indoors.

Stretched out on his large navy sofa, laptop on his lap, headphones on, Josh logs on to his game.

"You're late, man," one of his friends says.

"Yeah, I got caught up with a stray dog."

"Sounds like a drag," another says.

"Yeah," says Josh, although it hadn't been.

They set about storming the castle. Their guild was on day three of a quest into the Mines of Talblazia.

"Come on, Josh," says his teammate. "You just let Jimbro die. You gotta lock in."

But Josh was distracted. He'd opened a new browser tab and was looking at online neighborhood groups, reading through forum posts of stolen bikes, a lost rabbit, and furniture for sale. There was no post from someone missing their dog.

Brushing his teeth the following morning, he thinks of the dog and raises the bathroom blind to look for it. No sign of the dog, but the sky is blue, Chicago Cubs blue, with big fluffy white clouds that gleam brilliantly at the edges. Is the sky usually so vivid? It's beautiful. He goes to close the blind again, but then decides to keep it open.

Leaving his house, he keeps an eye out for the dog. The world is full of people walking their dogs this morning. At the bus stop, a particularly friendly black lab strains at his leash to sniff Josh's leg. Josh reaches to pet the dog.

"Sorry about that, he's just saying hello," says the owner

"No problem, I love dogs," says Josh.

"Have one of your own?" asks the man.

Josh has his phone out in a flash and shows the man the photo he'd snapped the night before. Josh is going to explain that he just found the dog, but before he can —

"Oh yes, you can always tell the bond between a dog and their person," the man says. "Fine looking pup. What's his name?"

"Goat," says Josh in a moment of inspiration.

"Goat?"

"Yes."

"Goat, the dog?" the man asks, raising an amused eyebrow. "G.O.A.T., like Greatest Of All Time?"

"No. Goat, like he eats everything, including the packaging."

Sitting on the bus, Josh gets the photo out again. He zooms in on Goat's face. How is it possible that it looks like the dog is smiling?

"Cute dog," the woman sitting next to him says.

And, it's lucky that she says something, as Josh is so engrossed in the photo that he is about to miss his stop. He flashes her a smile; she is pretty cute, too.

The rich, earthy aroma of coffee brewing permeates the small cafe as Josh waits in line. Plants trail across the ceiling in elaborate macramé slings. Their shiny leaves twist green and gold, like jungle vines.

"How's it going, man?" asks the barista.

"Hey, what's up?" Josh says, taken aback, the barista doesn't usually greet him. Then realizes his earbuds are still in his pocket. "I like the new plants."

"Plants? Those have always been there," the barista says, eyebrows furrowed for a second before he switches back to smiley. "Just the usual today: coffee and two percent? Can I get you anything else?"

"A hazelnut shot," he says, surprising himself.

Josh is just finishing the drink as he arrives at work. It is delicious, sweet, and creamy with notes of toasted nuts. He resolves to try all the syrup flavors. He tips his head back to drain the cup, and as he does, the tops of the skyscrapers are visible. Shining structures of steel and glass stretch way above him, reflecting the vibrant sky.

It occurs to him as he microwaves his lunch that there are no computer screens to protect from glare in the office kitchen, and the east exposure would mean a view over Lake Michigan. To check his hypothesis, he slides his thumb and forefinger between two slats in the blind. Through the peep-hole is a glimpse of azure shimmering water. Hoisting the blinds open, he feels cheated, like removing the linoleum on the floor to discover the original cherry hardwood under-neath. The blue of the lake transitions from an almost Caribbean color to the deepest navy. He doesn't take his lunch back to his desk; he eats looking at the view. Maybe next week, he'll go out for lunch and sit on a bench in Grant Park.

"Happy Friday! Oh, you opened the blinds. Good call!" beams Gabi, passing through. She bumps the Conference Room door open with her hip, her hands full, carrying a large platter of fresh fruit. "Michigan strawberries are in season! Best time of the year!" She is gone before he can reply.

Later that day, on the way home, he stops at the grocery store to stock up on ready meals. He buys a couple of cans of dog food and some treats in case Goat comes back. There is a display touting fresh Michigan strawberries, and Josh buys a punnet. On the walk home, he feels the evening sun warm on his skin. He whistles a song that was big when he was in high school, and decides to eat his dinner on the back deck to keep an eye out for Goat.

His deck doesn't get much use. He doesn't have furniture out there, but there's an upturned crate that works as a chair. He balances the microwave meal on his lap and puts the strawberries down by his side. The setting sun makes long shadows and bathes his neighborhood in golden light. The cicadas sing insistently, and the rich, earthy smell of grilled meat wafts through the air. A couple of doors down, someone is playing Motown classics, and squeals of laughter from children playing in a nearby sprinkler make Josh recall times he felt that free.

The sweet burst of the strawberries is a revelation. Crimson red, each one more delicious than the last. Gabi was right. She is a good egg, always trying to help people. She has good instincts.

When Josh finishes eating, he doesn't get up. There's no sign of Goat, but he's in no rush. He stays seated on the crate, just listening to the sounds of his neighborhood, watching the shadows lengthen and the light dim, his jaw unclenches. A squirrel bounds across the fence, birds gather high on a wire, and Josh remains perfectly still, taking it all in. His breathing slows, and his shoulders relax. A soft breeze stirs in the cooler air, bringing the sweet scent of a rose bush in bloom. When the sun finally sets and the shadows blanket the scene, he feels as he once did after an ex-girlfriend persuaded him to try meditation—fully present and in his body.

The usual divide between him and the world is diminished. He takes a long, slow breath before getting up to take his empty dinner carton over to the bins. Pulsing fireflies seem to follow him.

Almost immediately, a small dark shape appears to greet him.

Goat. Tail wagging.

"Hey, boy!"

Josh bends to pet the dog, who wags his tail so much at the reunion that his whole back half wags with it.

"Listen, we need to get you inside. I have food for you, and I can figure out what to do with you then."

Goat licks Josh's face, prompting Josh to laugh in delight, even as he squirms, wondering where that mouth has been.

"You can't be out on the street—they'll put you in the pound! Come on! This way!"

Josh starts a slow jog back to his apartment door, checking over his shoulder. To his delight, Goat follows, thinking this is a great game.

Back inside, a frenetic Goat tries to get on the sofa, at which point Josh realizes that the dog is truly filthy.

"Goat, no offense, but you smell."

In Josh's shower, he checks the temperature and the water pressure and moves the showerhead over every inch of the dog, who lets him, gazing up at him with serious eyes. Josh is intent on the clean and doesn't see this. He works the soap into a thick foam, massaging it through Goat's fur, before rinsing it off. The lather lands in big wet splats on the shower floor.

Goat allows Josh to clean his paws, lifting each one in turn. It's at this point, as Josh sits on his bathroom floor, the street dirt spiraling down the plughole, Goat's front left paw in his hand, that their eyes meet. Goat's big brown eyes are wide and solemn.

"Aw, I know. It's going to be OK."

An hour after that, both Josh and Goat are soaked through. There are puddles throughout the apartment, and four towels are soiled to such a degree that Josh wonders if they will ever be clean again. Josh will be cleaning fur out of the shower drain for the next month, but Goat is clean. When Josh dries him with yet another towel, it turns out his coat isn't a dull grey at all; it is a sumptuous black flecked with bronze and chestnut.

"You're a handsome guy, Goat."

Josh has missed the evening's questing in the Mines of Talblazia, so instead the two of them settle into the sofa and watch a movie.

"Tomorrow morning I'll take you to the vet," says Josh, biting the inside of his cheek, as an ache starts to grow inside. "And we'll see who you belong to." He knows it's the right thing to do.

Goat is lying next to Josh, his chin on Josh's chest. Goat's eyelids grow heavy and slide shut.

"You probably are the greatest of all time," whispers Josh.

At the Saturday walk-in vet clinic, Josh chats with other pet owners in the waiting room. They laugh and share pet names and ages. They are all good girls and good boys, and the receptionist is generous with the treats. It's only as he is called through that he realizes he has left his phone at home. He hasn't missed it at all. He is wondering who Goat's owner is and if they are kind to him.

The vet explains after an examination that Goat has no microchip, but that he is already spayed, and congratulates Josh on his new dog. Things are moving fast for Josh, but he has never felt more sure about anything. There's no way he is taking Goat to the pound, and anyway, they already feel like a team. On the way out of the vet's, Josh spots a familiar face from the office. She's looking in the window of a gift store.

"Morning, Gabi," he says.

She looks so different out of work, relaxed, her smile gives him confidence. "Did you do something different with your hair?"

"Josh!" says Gabi in surprise with a wide smile, touching her hair. "I didn't know you had a dog."

"Yeah, I just got him."

"He's such a cutie," says Gabi, crouching to say hello to Goat, who licks her face.

"He likes you," says Josh. Goat has good taste.

"I like him too! How would you feel about bringing him into the office? I've seen that help morale in the workplace."

"Yeah! I definitely can."

"Is he a rescue?" Gabi asks.

"He *is* a rescue," says Josh with a big smile, watching Gabi and Goat together.

Every time Gabi pays attention to Josh, Goat nudges her hand with his nose as a reminder to pet him. Conversation is much easier this way, Josh finds, sharing the focus, not having all eyes on him.

"I picked up some strawberries after you mentioned them in the office yesterday - great recommendation."

"Oh, you did? Aren't they the best?" she says, turning to

face him, still smiling, her nose crinkling in a charming way. "I never know if anyone listens to my recommendations."

"Well, you've got one person here now who will for sure."

Gabi laughs and goes back to petting Goat, who is insisting upon it.

It occurs to him that it feels good to have someone to recommend things to him and with whom to share discoveries. Josh takes a deep breath and, on the exhale, not overthinking, not giving himself time to back out, he says, "Hey Gabi, are you free to grab a coffee?"

"What's that?" she says, turning to face him, her eyebrows raised in an open question.

She didn't hear! The familiar ache in his stomach starts to rise, and his heartbeat quickens. It's a terrible idea. He swallows and feels adrift, far from shore, but when he looks at her—actually meets her gaze, and holds it—the discomfort recedes. He is in the moment, heart and mind, when he repeats the question.

"Gabi, do you want to go get a coffee?"

"I'd love to!"

"Alright!" says Josh, his grin is so huge that on a normal day, he might feel self-conscious about it, but an unfamiliar rush is going through him, and his mind is elsewhere.

As the three of them head off to the coffee shop together, chatting and laughing at Goat's antics, he remembers how much he enjoyed the hazelnut syrup and makes a mental note to ask Gabi if she's had it before. He can't wait to see if she thinks it's delicious too.

LIKE FATHER, LIKE SON

A LOUD BANG from the garden, followed by children's screams, stopped Rose and her father-in-law's conversation dead. Rose froze midway through putting five candles on her daughter's cake, and her eyes locked with those of the older man.

"Just balloons popping on the rose bushes in the wind, good screams, laughter," she said.

"Jesus," said the older man in a quiet growl. They were alone in the kitchen, but he kept his voice low. "Rose, it's getting too dangerous. Time for you to bow out."

"Nonsense, David. You said it yourself, the stakes have never been higher." Rose looped a tress of black hair back behind her ear and stood up straight.

"Yes, but that was before I knew how deep you'd get. You're a mother! You're too exposed. And there's more." He leaned in closer, his angular face inches from hers, "We have reason to believe there's a mole."

The kitchen door flew open, and in came a disheveled man dressed in cargo shorts and a Hawaiian shirt. He had a scruffy beard and a big grin.

"Sweetheart, I've got twelve five-year-old girls out there desperate for cake! How's it coming along?" He swooped an arm around David. "Oh, hey, Dad. I didn't see you come in. Very sensible hiding out, away from the madding crowd. What are you two talking about?"

"Oh, just traffic on the inner bypass. Think you can keep them at bay with some lemonade? All that bouncing, surely they're thirsty by now." She passed him a tray of filled flowery paper cups from the fridge and closed it with a hip bump. "Don't let them breach the perimeter!"

"Don't worry"—Simon dipped and kissed her on the cheek—"I won't let anything happen to this family. Just don't be too long with the cake." He pantomimed bracing for battle. "Once more into the breach!"

"Godspeed!" she called after him, playing along. As the door shut behind him, she turned to her father-in-law, serious now. "A mole? What do we know?"

"Not much. It's sure to be someone from ACT. Impossible to chalk up all their wins to luck alone. They're one step ahead of us; a dawn raid at one of their hideouts on Monday found the place completely cleared out, no fingerprints. There's a leak."

"Mia? That weasel Anton?"

"No one is above suspicion."

Her jaw set. "One more drop. With this last puzzle piece, we can exact maximum damage. We can end them. It's what this has all been for."

David let out a big sigh and raked his hand through his silver hair. "Damn it, Rose. Your bravery is putting us all in danger. This is the last one. I'll be in touch."

Rose and Simon were just back from their honeymoon when David approached her about joining the Ring. David told her he knew Simon wasn't made of the right stuff; he was too credulous, not observant enough. But she was cut from a different cloth. He had watched her closely and recognized her mettle immediately. She noticed subtle changes and remembered little details. She was resourceful. She was determined. He sometimes wondered what she saw in his son and was just grateful that opposites seemed to attract.

When Simon and Rose were dating, they drove from London to stay with Simon's parents in the Cotswolds for the holidays. Rose had no family, and so holidays with Simon's family became the norm. Simon's mom was old-fashioned and insisted that they not share a bed until they were married.

One day, David found them in a room together and read what had been going on from his son's disheveled appearance, flushed face, and evasive gaze. His future daughter-in-law was just as calm and breezy as ever. There had been a pair of underwear on the floor. Naturally, he spotted them when he walked into the room. She moved them, spirited them away. He didn't see how. A sleight of hand.

And there was Rose's ambiguous ethnicity: she was hard to pin down, a shape-shifter. She was pretty, not so much as to attract attention, but easy enough on the eye to use to her advantage. She was fit too and disciplined. David wasn't sure how far she went on her early morning runs while Simon slept, but he noticed river mud on her shoes after one morning run, which meant at least seven miles. And she was a whiz with technology. She had helped David recover saved files and unfreeze his computer multiple times.

But the point that convinced David was Rose's steadfast commitment to the then-new government, Commanding Tribune. They were building back a stronger Britain and looking forward to a bright future. And if David's son wasn't cut out to join the Ring, then at least his new daughter-in-law was.

Rose felt Simon had much more in common with his father than David realized. They were both fiercely protective of their family and hands-on dads. When Simon became a dad, he cried, holding their newborn, overcome with emotion. He swore to her that he would do anything to keep them safe. Rose believed him; he was just like his dad.

At first, she was simply an anonymous link in a chain. David had insisted on shielding her from anything more dangerous, so no direct contact at first. She simply collected dead drops and moved them to their next collection point. She would never forget the thrill of liberating her first USB stick from its home, taped to the underside of a park bench. She sat on the bench, checked that the coast was clear, and leaned over to do up a shoelace. She saw the white finger of plastic, and as if holding the bench to rise again, she smoothly palmed it.

She badgered David to give her more to do. She wanted more impact, which meant more risk. Over time, he reluctantly relented, and her fieldwork evolved into dealing with other Ring agents face-to-face.

Rose was steps from home, returning from the morning school run, when she received David's typically cryptic instruction text. *Lovely day for a walk, three ducks on the pond, and a sparrow in the oak.*

She did an about-turn and headed to the park. On the way, she received an uncharacteristic second text from David. *Be careful.*

It was a looming grey day, decidedly not a lovely day for a walk. Low clouds hung like suspicion in the air, and there was an eerie quiet in the street. The only sound was her footsteps on the grey flagstone sidewalk. Nevertheless, she carefully checked that she wasn't being followed. She counted the benches as she entered the park and stopped to sit on the third one. A jogger appeared, as if from nowhere, giving her a small start. His footstrike in the gravel made crunching sounds that faded as he ran away from her.

How did she not hear him coming? A chill went through her, and she pulled her long wool coat closer around her. Today was not the day to be off her game.

Another man was seated two benches down, reading a newspaper. Who still reads a newspaper these days? Rose positioned herself to watch him while looking like she was checking her phone. After a few minutes, he got up and left. Alone in the park now, she was wearing slip-on ankle boots, so no pretend shoelace tying today. Instead, she dropped her phone on the path, bending to pick it up, she scanned the underside of the bench and saw a yellow pencil taped up. More recently, the Ring switched from USBs to microfilm. Rose put her phone back in her pocket, allowing her coat to spill over part of the bench while her fingers worked underneath to get the pencil.

She rolled the pencil between her fingers in her pocket as she left the park, still careful that she was not followed. Step one, the three ducks, was complete. Next, the more dangerous step two, the sparrow in the oak. She allowed herself a small smile. The file she would deliver tonight would change everything.

· · ·

The Commanding Tribune's early years saw a regrettable rise in domestic terrorism: small, disorganized, stochastic attacks. The intelligence efforts of the Ring made inroads into neutralizing the threat, but had forced a lean and more organized group underground. The group, Against Commanding Tribune, known as ACT, had been a thorn in the government's side for nearly a decade. David recruited Rose into the Ring around that time. And they were now just one puzzle piece away from ending ACT. It would be the Ring's single biggest achievement.

That evening, Rose left her daughter and Simon at home on the sofa, a sit-com on the TV, and a fire in the grate, as she headed out for step two. She told them she was popping out, that she forgot to get pasta. Simon offered to go. Of course he did. She told him not to worry, to relax, and she wanted to stretch her legs. She kissed them both before heading out into the dark.

David, alone, paced in his London *pied-à-terre*, and checked his phone again: no messages. It had been hours. Why did he let her talk him into this? What if something happened to her? Simon wouldn't understand. He would never forgive him. No, his son could never discover her involvement, and that David had recruited her.

David knew firsthand that the danger was real. His hand went to his shoulder, the site of a gunshot wound from a few years ago—an unseen sniper in the bushes. He was lucky that day; maybe Rose wouldn't be so lucky.

David found himself gnawing on a hangnail and scoffed. She was out there, and so was the mole. Something didn't smell right. He looked at his watch; he could still make it. He went to the safe and took out his pistol, grabbed his coat, and strode out of the flat.

The meeting spot, the "oak", was a disused public restroom by the canal. Rose turned off the brightly lit pavement, with its comforting hum of foot traffic and cars, down the steps onto the towpath and into the darkness. A small animal rustled through some leaves in the scrubby woodland on her left. The moon, between silver-hemmed clouds, sent a shimmer of light over the canal to her right. A group of three barges moored together, low to the water, felt like a conspiracy. In the black of night, her senses heightened. Her rubber-soled shoes allowed her to pad along silently. At the restroom, she hesitated at the door. She felt someone behind her and turned quickly.

Her eyes struggled to make sense of the dark. She stood for a few moments, holding her breath to hear better. Her heartbeat was in her ears. No one up to any good was around the canal at night; drug addicts and other miscreants were known to gather here. She waited another couple of minutes. Her body was perfectly still, sure of the feeling that there was someone there, until deciding it must be some punk kid who'd come to score.

She pivoted and walked into the run-down building.

A pale sliver of moonlight sliced through the restroom. Rose slid into the space, keeping her back to the wall. She rolled the pencil between her fingers in her pocket. A figure stepped out of the blackness, his pale face stood out against his dark clothes and hair. It was Anton.

"Ah, Rose, I was hoping you'd come," he said, folding his arms. "You know they think there's a mole?"

"I heard," she said.

"Who do you think it could be?"

"No idea, Anton. Maybe it's you."

He scoffed.

"Let's just get this over with," she said, rolling her eyes. She held the pencil out, but he didn't take it.

"I noticed some very curious patterns in your drops, Rose, so I took the liberty of following you."

She shifted her weight onto her other foot.

"Imagine my surprise when I saw you with a known ACT operative this afternoon," he said.

"You're mistaken."

"Oh no, Rose, I don't think I am. After you left, I neutralized him and recovered the microfilm." He uncrossed his arms and took a tiny square from his shirt pocket. "This one, the one that is supposed to be in that pencil."

Rose's shoulders slumped. She put the pencil back in her pocket and ran her finger over its sharp point.

"Why Rose? You know that your husband will be arrested; they'll never believe he wasn't involved. Your child will be taken away."

"Anton, just take me, leave my family out of this. Simon is innocent."

"But, why risk it all?"

Rose sighed before she spoke. "When I came to this country, I was alone. I thought ACT was doing the right thing. I thought I was fighting for freedom."

"And now?"

"I just don't know anymore," she said. "So much bloodshed. So many lies. What's the point of any of it? None of us is safer, none of us is freer. Do you feel safer, Anton, with the work the Ring is doing?"

"You shouldn't feel safe right now, Rose," he said as he took a step toward her.

They were interrupted by a movement at the door and the outline of a man in the doorway.

"Excellent work, Anton."

Rose recognized David's voice with dismay.

David entered the room slowly, pistol pointing at Rose.

"David, I didn't know you were working tonight," Anton said.

"All the Ring's top brass have been working overtime on this mole issue. I heard everything. Well done. Who else knows about this?"

"Just me, I wanted to confront her to confi—" David fired the weapon, but not at Rose. Anton slid to the floor.

Rose gasped and pressed her body closer to the wall.

"I guess I've always known." The barrel of the gun was pointing at her.

"I'm so sorry, David," she said.

"You put on quite the show to get me to recruit you." He shook his head. "You were the common link every time the intel was bad. I didn't want to believe it. Fixing my computer, you were stealing files. Yes?"

Rose lowered her head.

"It was obvious. Why would a woman like you go for Simon?"

Rose thrust her face to meet his gaze in the dim light, "Simon is a wonderful husband and father. I have grown to love him. He loves me. We are a family."

"You put them at risk!"

"They were never at risk. I would have died for them. Just as I risked myself for you!"

"What are you talking about?"

"The shoulder injury you told us you got from falling off your bike! I was there. I was the reason that sniper didn't get a kill shot."

"You saved me?" he asked.

"And I'd do it again. This family is everything to me."

"God help me, Rose," David sighed and lowered the gun. "I believe you. Obviously, tonight was your last mission for the Ring."

He bent to retrieve the microfilm from Anton's body. "We need to get this to the Ring to complete the drop as planned. I'll take care of that. The information on this will end ACT for good. Do you understand?" As he said that, he met her eyes.

"Yes, but the real microfilm is here. She passed him the pencil. I never handed it over to ACT. I just wanted all this to be over."

"Rose, I need to know that you are done," he said.

"I'm done. It's over," she said.

"Will they look for me?" she asked.

"No, but they will be surprised to learn that Anton was the mole," David said, lifting Anton under his armpits. We have to get him out of here. Grab his legs."

Rose did as she was asked.

"I won't let anything happen to this family," he said.

Simon and David are so alike, Rose thought, not for the first time.

LOVE SPELLS

STAN WIELDED his comb like a scalpel to make a perfect part in his grey hair. There wasn't as much of it as there used to be, but enough to be styled, and tonight it was important that he looked his best. A dab of pomade was the finishing touch. He tucked in his blue button-down—selected for this evening because Gladys had always told him that it brought out the color of his eyes.

Last Christmas, his daughter gave him a bottle of cologne in a jade-green glass bottle with an ornate gold stopper. It sat unopened and full of promise. Why not? he thought.

He tore off the wrapping and pumped a burst of the fragrance on each side of his neck. This was no time for half measures, so he sprayed again on each side. After a short coughing fit, he popped a breath mint into his mouth and put the box in his cardigan pocket.

Before he left his unit, he picked up a silver-framed photo of a woman. He had taken the shot during a day out, two decades earlier. She was in her early 50s, still striking, bare legs outstretched on a chequered picnic blanket. They had shared a bottle of wine and napped in the shade of a sycamore tree. She gazed over her shoulder directly into the lens, but her twinkly eyes and wide, generous smile were for the man behind the camera—a moment of electric connection in a lifetime of togetherness captured in the snap of a shutter.

"Well, love. You would be proud of me. I hadn't felt ready until now." He cleared his throat. "I'll let you know how it goes. Love you always, Gladys."

"You look nice, Stan," said the recreation therapist in the hallway. "Glad to see you out for a change. I trust we are going to the same place—board game night?"

"We are indeed!" Stan, more pep in his step than usual, opened the heavy fireproof door to the common room and stood by, chest out, to allow the young woman through.

"Oh, you smell nice!" she said, having to pass close by him to get through the door.

Once inside, he scanned the busy room. There were half a dozen or so tables, each with a board game in progress. Residents rolling dice, dealing cards, and noting down scores with the assiduous care of a CPA.

Chatter hummed in the air, and his heart beat in his throat. Was she there?

"Stan, over here!"

He turned to the sound of the call and beamed. There she was: a crown of curls, big round glasses, a fluffy pink sweater, and rosy cheeks.

She had saved him a seat next to her.

"Cora, you look very fetching this evening."

Her friends made wide eyes at each other.

During the Scrabble game, their legs touched under the

table. Stan jerked away as though electrocuted, but Cora's leg followed to nestle again. His face grew warm.

She played K-I-S-S.

He played P-R-E-T-T-Y.

"Double word score, thirty-four points," she said, pencil scribbling in the notebook.

After the game, Stan stood up.

"Cora, may I walk you back to your room?"

"It's a lovely evening, perhaps we might walk outside?"

He offered her an arm, which she took and squeezed him in closer.

As they walked through the grounds, cicadas serenading them in the warm summer air, he felt the time was right. He retrieved the box from his pocket.

"May I offer you a breath mint, Cora?"

She knew what that meant. Her look grew coquettish. "Why, yes, you may, Stan."

REFLECTIONS

THE NIGHT before his father's funeral, Daniel Carlson Jr. met up with a school friend, Max, in a Wicker Park brick-front dive bar with a flickering neon Old Style sign buzzing in the window. Daniel arrived first, crossing a sticky floor to grab a high-top table and a couple of stools near the bar. When Max arrived, they hugged like brothers.

"I'm so sorry, man. How are you holding up?" Max said, his blue eyes full of concern.

"You know, it still doesn't feel real. Just the admin alone: death certificates, closing his accounts, getting the house ready to sell, funeral arrangements, flowers—" Daniel shook his head "—it's a lot. Much easier when Mom went. It all just fell to him then."

"Did you manage to get time off work?"

"Four days. Deals don't take time off for grief. I'll be lucky if they don't schedule a conference call during the funeral."

"I think they'd understand. Even investment bankers are human some of the time."

"It's just brutal timing. We're about to do a massive transaction and I'm chained to my laptop until it's through."

"Dude," said Max, knowing it was pointless trying to persuade his ambitious friend to take a step back from work. "How's Beth holding up?"

Daniel let out a low moan at the mention of his little sister, whose apartment he was staying at while he was back in town. "Not good."

Both men took a sip of beer.

"I've been working on Dad's eulogy," Daniel said, the words hardly seemed real. "What memories do you have of him?"

"Your dad was amazing! Not many did more for people than your dad. That man was a pillar of the community!"

"Yeah, but as a man, as a father, I mean. Do you have any stories?"

For a fleeting moment, Max looked trapped in crosshairs. "He wasn't around much, was he?" And then he remembered, "Oh, well, when those girls went missing, he was all over it, leading search parties. I was in a group he led, and that man was so engaged, anyone would think it was his own child who had gone missing."

Daniel frowned. "I don't think I can include that. How to make a funeral even more depressing? Remind the whole town about the three girls who went missing fifteen years ago."

"Yeah, not a crowd pleaser." Max leaned in. "My mom put us on lockdown that summer. She didn't want us to be next. There were missing posters everywhere with that photo of that one girl. Braids, braces, and that dolphin necklace."

"Right, right, Dolphin Girl! And then those other two girls, a few years later."

"Crazy to think that all happened in sleepy Glenville.

They never found her, and they never caught the guy who did it. Must have been a real sicko."

They weren't late leaving the bar. Daniel still needed to work on the eulogy, and he didn't like leaving Beth alone for too long—an old habit from the days of the missing girls.

The next day, Daniel, dressed in a somber black suit, adjusted his tie in the bathroom mirror of his younger sister's apartment. He splashed water on his face and smoothed some of it over his fresh-from-the-barber dark hair. Black suit, black tie, shadows under his brown eyes—his father's eyes. He gripped the sink with both hands and leaned in as if to say something of utmost importance to his likeness. He searched the eyes of the young man in front of him. So, this is how he looked, all dressed up for his father's funeral.

He slipped a hand into the silk-lined pocket of his bespoke suit to check the eulogy he'd finally completed was still safe. The bones of the text had been easy enough to write. Most of the people at the service could have written it.

His father, Daniel Carlson Sr., was well-known and had amassed an impressive list of accomplishments. As a younger man, he had been in the military, achieved the rank of First Lieutenant, and served overseas before settling down with Daniel and Beth's mom. With young kids, his dad started what became a very successful business, Carlson Construction. The company was a preferred local contractor and an important employer in the community. He had served as a Rotary board member, was active in the church, had been generous with donations of money, and even found time to coach Little League.

But the intimate details, the tear-jerking morsels he knew people expected, were more elusive. After his mother had passed, when he and Beth were in high school, Daniel felt his father's distance more than ever. The man was rarely at home, and Daniel found himself taking on a parental role for Beth.

He checked his chunky Swiss watch. It was time to leave.

"Beth, you ready?" He slipped on an expensive wool coat. "We have to get going."

His sister, just out of college, sometimes looked like she could still be in high school. He found her sitting on the couch. She was dressed and ready to go, but was mannequin-still and stared unfocused ahead of her—an out-of-place blob of dark matter among the chintzy pinks and turquoise she'd chosen for her surroundings. Her long, dark eyelashes and delicate retroussé nose gave her a baby bird-like effect.

He didn't want to rush her out of whatever cocoon she had created for herself. Their mom had died almost exactly a decade earlier. She had taken a fall while doing yardwork and hit her head. The siblings were alone now.

"I can't believe he's gone," she said, motionless. Fat tears slipped down her cheeks.

It was a good hour's drive from Beth's apartment to the Glenville Covenant Church, where their father had been an elder. As they left the city, skyscrapers gave way to low-rise apartment blocks, which gradually gave way to single-family homes. The neighborhoods turned into fields, and small lakes splotched the flat landscape, signaling they were close to home.

It was a bleak October day, and the grey sky hung low as if the clouds themselves had assembled to mourn.

Daniel drove the unremarkable sedan he rented and was grateful that the traffic was light.

"Thanks for doing his eulogy, Danny," Beth said. "I don't think I'd be able to get through it."

"Well, let's see if I can." He paused, weighing whether to share the next part. "You know, it was difficult to remember specific examples of when Dad was home." He pulled up to a stop sign and checked both ways before pulling out, stealing a look at her expression.

"Well, I mean, Dad was wonderful, so I know that he probably wasn't around as much as other dads, but that's because he was out supporting the whole town. You got that in there, right?" Her tone grew urgent. "That he was on the board of Rotary and all the money they raised?"

"Yeah, of course."

"And he took the Little League team on to win the district championship?"

"Yes, that's in there too, of course, everyone remembers that one."

Beth smiled.

"And the Thanksgiving meal he organized with the food pantry. Remember him up on the stage, carving up all those turkeys? He got pretty quick at it by the end!" he said.

Beth gave a little laugh that turned watery at the end.

Daniel chewed his lip. His flight was booked for the next day, heading back out east to his job. Was she going to be OK?

He didn't bring up the rough patch his parents had gone through around his fourteenth birthday; no point upsetting Beth with that memory. His mom had seemed perpetually agitated. The first question she asked his Dad when he got home from work was where he'd been. Daniel had seen her go through his pockets on more than one occasion and even the trunk of his car. They argued a lot during that time. Daniel assumed she suspected an affair.

A few miles down the road, he said, "Look, Beth, Lincoln Middle. Home of the PrairieWolves!"

They were silent as their old school slid by them.

"Beth, do you remember when Dolphin Girl went missing?"

"Sure," said Beth. "So many posters. She was gone, but also all around us, her face on every lamppost. It was so eerie. I knew she wasn't coming back when they found the bodies of the two other girls out in the woods. What were their names? Sasha someone, and I don't remember the other girl."

"Sasha sounds right. I don't remember the other girl's name either. So sad."

"I know you were worried about me then," said Beth. "You thought you were being subtle following me home from school, but I knew you were looking out for me."

"Ha! No alternative career as a spy for me then," he said.

Arriving at the church, they found the lot full and had to drive a couple of hundred feet further before they found a spot on the grassy verge at the side of the road.

"It looks like the whole town turned out," Daniel said.

They sat in the car for a moment before getting out. There were people from the church, his army days, folks from the town council, from the tennis club, friends, former employees, and neighbors.

As they got out of the car, they surveyed it all. Trees lifted their bare branches to the heavens, their leaves piling up in dead, brown piles where they had been blown against the church. Streams of people in dark clothes made their way, tributaries forming a black river into the church. The fall air was damp and musty. A heartbeat caught in Daniel's throat.

Beth said under her breath, "Wow".

"Yeah," Daniel said and put his arm across her slim shoulders. Beth leaned into him. The siblings walked into the church behind the coffin. The man who'd loomed so large now in a wooden box—close, but unreachable.

After the service, the clouds had lifted. The world looked brighter, and Daniel found he could breathe easier. The service itself had been a blur of standing and sitting and singing on cue and en masse. He had gotten through it like a robot, and now it was over. Of course, Beth had wept throughout. Daniel had been expecting that.

The reception was to be held at the tennis club. Beth's best friend had gone into full mother-hen mode and insisted on taking Beth to the reception herself. Daniel, after checking that was what his sister wanted, found himself alone and decided to stop by their childhood home on his way to the reception. He knew it would be empty, but wanted to check on the state of the old house. He hoped to decompress there. And perhaps even feel close to his father.

It was a pleasant drive, just a little way out of the town, past a small lake and some woodland. He pulled up at the house, which was situated on an acre of land. All was still.

He wandered around the yard first. The grass was patchy and brown. A giant elm tree still bore the tire swing he'd loved as a kid. Rainwater and dead leaves had pooled inside the tire, but he didn't hesitate to step onto it. He looked anew at the house with its proud gable, blue wooden clapboard siding, and a wrap-around porch. His mother used to hang bushy ferns in the spring, which would stay lush and green all summer if she watered them twice on the hot days.

Right then, swinging, he remembered walking up the path from school one day. His heart had skipped when he saw his father at home, a rare event. He saw the scene as if fresh. His father, by the house, with his broad back to him. Daniel didn't call out to him; he wanted to surprise him, so his father hadn't heard the boy approach. Daniel Carlson Sr. was hunched over a trapped raccoon. The animal had plagued the family for weeks, chewing through screens and knocking over trash cans, and scattering garbage. Just feet from his father, Daniel was about to say something when his father lifted a length of piping and brought it down onto the animal. The raccoon shrieked in pain—until the third or fourth blow.

Just as then, he felt ringing in his ears, a hollowing in his stomach, and knew he could never share this particular experience with Beth. He hopped down from the swing, took a deep breath, and walked up the creaky steps to the porch.

He cupped his hands to the glass to peer in through the living room window. The room had been emptied, and the furniture had been donated per his instructions. It was all so dated that even his sister, who was sentimental and fresh out of college with no cash, didn't want to take it.

On a whim, he tried the front door, which, to his surprise, opened easily. Inside, the house smelled of mustiness mixed with the old fireplace. Dust shone suspended in the air. His dress shoes slapped on the newly rugless wooden floorboards. The place was a time capsule; there had been no renovations or changes since his mother passed 15 years ago. Cherry wood kitchen cabinets and stainless steel appliances in the kitchen. He wondered if they'd need to make updates to sell the property.

Upstairs, he checked the ceilings for signs of water damage and stood in his childhood bedroom where his bed would have been. He thought of the times he'd comforted Beth during storms when their father was out late at night.

She would knock on his door, hugging her teddy, and he would let her in, and they'd hide in his closet playing cards to distract her until the storm had passed. He didn't know what he expected to feel, but he was keen to escape a rising sadness in his chest. It drove him down the hallway to his parents' room.

Their room was handsome, of generous proportions, and, with all the furniture removed, the craftsman-style details in the baseboards and molding stood out. He paused, leaning on the door frame, and felt a wave of melancholy wash over him. So much life had happened in this house.

His father had painted the cherry hardwood floors himself. The handiwork was flawless. Except there was a rough patch in one spot, which would have been under his father's side of the bed.

On closer inspection, the floorboards weren't quite flush there. He pushed on one of the ends, and to his surprise, it levered up a half inch. He worked at it until the floorboard came loose. He shone his smartphone flashlight in the hole. There was a small space under the floorboard with a battered tin box inside.

His heart rushed to his throat—something of his father's, some secret treasure. He opened the box to find a mess of metal chain and faded pink fabric. He teased the tangle apart until he was holding three distinct items in his hand: a pink hair bow, a silver chain bracelet with the name 'Sasha' engraved in cursive, and a dolphin necklace.

Dolphin girl, Sasha. The third missing girl.

Daniel felt a pounding behind his eyes, and his insides grew into a hot and curdled mass which rose rapidly into his throat. Propelled to his parents' bathroom, he hurtled toward the toilet and got there just in time to expel the rush of burning vomit. Dizzy, he sat on the cool tile floor, his throat stung from bile, eyes unfocused. The significance of what he found crawled over his flesh.

His father had been so keen to help out with the search for the girls. That made more sense now. He knew what the right thing to do was. He also knew that Beth must never know about this. He considered the ramifications for his job. He would be encouraged to leave. His thoughts churned.

The phone in his hand started ringing and vibrating, which brought him back to the present. It had been an hour since the service.

"Dan, where you at? We're all at the tennis club. Everyone's asking for you."

"Maxie," Daniel was surprised at how easily his voice sounded normal, smooth even. "Just checking over the old house, one last look. I'm heading over now."

Daniel got up from the bathroom floor. He walked to the sink and turned the tap. He smoothed some of it over his hair. Dark hair, dark suit—and his father's dark eyes. He looked paler now. He knew what he had to do.

Back in his parents' room, he replaced the items into the tin box, closing the lid with a click, and slid it into his pocket. He slotted the floorboard back in place, leaving it just as he had found it. He left the house without a backward look and drove back along the deserted road, toward the reception with his window down. The air felt good on his skin.

The car stirred up fall leaves in its wake, leaving them swirling. As he approached the grey calm lake, he took the box out of his pocket. He felt the weight of it, slowing down as the car drew alongside the water. With considerable effort, he hurled the box out of the moving car's window with as much force as he could muster. It landed twenty feet into the lake with a discreet splash. He watched it disappear beneath the surface. Ripples radiated from the place it landed. By the time the car was out of sight, the surface of the lake was smooth again.

A GREEK TRAGEDY

"AND SO, King Pyrrhus agreed to help the Greeks fight the Romans—" the cardigan-clad professor continued in nasal tones.

Clarissa was taking notes in her favorite class, The Hellenistic Age, when she was distracted by a small, dog-eared card poking out from her wallet. On it were six pictures of bulging gyros, each stamped haphazardly with a checkmark. It was the last day of the 'get your seventh free!' promotion at the best sandwich shop in town, Pita The Action. *Open until 3 pm on weekdays,* the small print read.

"—in which he was, as we know, very successful, but sustaining so much loss, suffering so many casualties, in each battle—"

Now here was an idea. Clarissa checked her watch; it would be tight, but she could make it across town and back to campus for afternoon lectures if he finished the class on time. Which, of course, he never did. Some students started discreetly packing up. She joined them, slipping her notebook into her backpack.

"—which led him to utter the astute observation, 'If we

are victorious in one more battle with the Romans, we shall be utterly ruined'."

More sounds of backpacks zipping and pens clicking. She could easily get a sandwich tomorrow, plenty of time in her schedule to do it then, but it was the last day of the promotion. Clarissa's stomach growled.

"—Thus giving us the immortal phrase 'a pyrrhic victory'!—"

Victory. With the promotion, she would be able to get a whole sandwich for free. She licked her lips. Chairs started to scrape.

"And that's where we'll leave things for today," the professor said, finally reading the room.

Clarissa slammed her laptop shut and jumped out of her seat. She had an hour; it would be tight. The first out of the door, she calculated bus versus walking times as she flew down the stairs and across the quad.

The bus won, even allowing for a five-minute wait at both ends. She arrived at the stop breathless just as a drizzle started.

Ten minutes later, there was no bus, the drizzle became a downpour, and traffic was at a near standstill. She reweighed her options, double-checked the maps app on her phone, and started a half-jog to the next bus stop, spurred on by saliva-inducing images of warm pita bread heaped with herbed chicken. Crossing a street in the rain, she slid off the slick curb, twisted her ankle, fell onto her knee, and dropped her phone screenside down so that it was webbed with spidery cracks when she turned it to see.

Drenched through, she brushed herself off and made it to the next bus stop, arriving at the same time as the bus that she would have caught had she stayed put. She found a seat, took off her heavy backpack full of textbooks, and rubbed her ankle, but her mind was on her sandwich.

The traffic was gridlocked.

"Come on, come on," she said under her breath, willing the bus forward. Her foot tapped out a rhythm in the tempo of adrenaline. At last, the road cleared and they started moving. The clock was ticking, but she could still make it as long as there was no line at the sandwich shop.

Clarissa could see the line outside Pita The Action from two hundred feet away as she got off the bus. She thought about turning back, but the welcoming blue and white striped awning, turned brilliant by the sun emerging from behind the clouds, felt like a sign to continue. It was only after ten minutes of standing in the queue, tantalized by the fragrance of warmed garlic and oregano, and the sound of meat sizzling on a hot plate, that she realized she had left her backpack on the bus.

A mental tally of the losses included her laptop, essential handwritten notes from the week's lectures, her keys, and her favorite water bottle. Oh well! She was next to be served. She would deal with her backpack later.

"Kalimera!" The rotund, gold chain-wearing owner gave the familiar greeting. "What can I get you?"

"I have the loyalty card," she said, holding it aloft like Prometheus offering his torch of fire to humanity. "Chicken gyro. Everything on it. To go, please."

Moments later, she was handed a warm bundle wrapped in foil, which she accepted with reverence, tucking it into the soft part of her inner elbow, as though it were a newborn king. She checked her watch. If she sprinted, she could bypass some of the traffic and pick up a bus where the route was clearer, but her ankle was starting to throb from the fall.

Out on the street, she was unable to fully bear weight on

her injured leg. The only way she could still make it back to campus in time was by taxi. She hailed a cab, noting that the price of the ride would be greater than the cost of the sandwich if she had paid for it.

Only when she had fastened her seatbelt across her did she gently open the wrapping. At once, she was struck by the familiar colors, red tomatoes, lush green lettuce, creamy tzatziki speckled with dill and cucumber, and the rich brown of roasted chicken all bundled in a cozy pita blanket. Warmth wafted up, carrying the smell to her. Gripping the sandwich, she took a large mouthful, which delivered every craveable flavor note at once: creamy, herby, tangy, meaty. Oily juices ran down between her fingers. She closed her eyes in utter bliss.

In the cocoon of the cab, raindrops racing down the window, her heart rate finally slowed. She bent to inspect her ankle, now radiating pain through her lower leg, only to see a trickle of blood she hadn't noticed before. At that moment, the cab stopped at a light outside a travel agency adorned with posters of the Greek Islands. *Visit us. Opa!*

THE BIG DAY

A WISE FRIEND once told Jessica that since physical feelings of nerves are almost identical to sensations of excitement, you can just tell your brain it's excitement that you are experiencing, and you'll feel less anxious.

That morning, in her childhood bedroom, as she dressed in the clothes she had set out for herself the night before, she tried this mindshift along with some deep breaths. On finding the method was somewhat successful, she made a mental note to text the friend later. They would want to know how her big day had gone too.

She opted for a natural makeup look, but she took extra care with her hair. She fixed her chestnut locks into a low chignon that accentuated her slim neck. Her fingers smoothed back wispy flyaways, securing them with a bobby pin, and she told herself that she was ready.

Or at least she would be, if she could speak to him before. She needed to ask him one more question to feel sure. This thought set her heart racing again, and she reminded herself to tell her brain it was excitement she was experiencing.

Her mother teared up when she saw her daughter

walking down the stairs. On the last step, Jess fell into the older woman's warm, tight, comforting embrace.

"I'm so proud of you, darling," she said, before releasing her so as not to get mascara on her daughter's white clothes. And then, sensing her trepidation, she put her hands onto Jessica's shoulders, looked deep into her eyes, and said as though she was implanting the thought itself, "You've got this."

Jessica had never been able to hide how she was feeling from her mother, but there was no need to share that she wouldn't be able to focus until she'd tied off that one loose end with him.

"I just don't want to let anyone down, Mom."

"You won't! You're ready." Her mother waved her off. "They're going to love you!"

The tires crunched over the gravel driveway of the elegant country house as she pulled up to the wedding venue. With her hand to her brow to shield her eyes from the bright sun, she scanned the scene, searching for him.

The gleaming Gilded Age mansion, the former abode of a New England financier, was modeled after a French château, but nothing compared to the celebrated gardens. Manicured conifers and a ribbon of cream flowers bordered the lawn that unfurled before her, mowed in stately stripes. The sweet fragrance of fresh-cut grass filled the air.

It was too early for guests, but the site hummed with the activity of preparation. Engrossed in their tasks, they paid no attention to her.

A team set folding chairs in rows and adorned each end with a pink bow for the ceremony on the lawn. One side of the marquee was pinned up, revealing waitstaff laying out cutlery on large round tables and a barman polishing glassware.

She spotted him by the floral arch. Tall, dark, and handsome. He was wearing a sharp suit and tucking a stray rose back into the trellis—so like him to notice the small details.

"Carlos," she called across the lawn. "We need to talk."

"Jess," he greeted her with a warm smile. "Congrats on your first wedding!"

"First of many, I hope," she said, grinning.

"I'm sure it will be. What's up?" he said.

"Just a question on timing—does the couple want the salad served with the entrée or before?"

"Before, please, Chef!"

Jessica gave him two thumbs up. She had known she would feel better after speaking with him. She donned her blue bandana over her hair, tying it in a low knot, as she strode toward the temporary kitchen set up in the marquee.

She didn't want to get too far ahead of herself; this was her first wedding catering contract after all, but if it went well, she knew Carlos would propose her for other events. This could be the beginning of a long partnership between them.

THE STUDENT

"HERE GOES NOTHING," Katy said to herself as she clicked 'send' on the weekly report her boss demanded but never looked at. She closed her laptop, slid it into her bag, and took her jacket off the back of her swivel chair. She would prefer to be asked to redo the report or even have it torn to shreds on a company-wide call, rather than it never see the light of day.

"Hey, Katy," her colleague, Lucy, called to her across the open-plan office. "Coming for drinks?"

"Can't," Katy knew they'd all still go for drinks without her. She was a bonus person, not an essential person. "I've signed up to do this tutoring for at-risk youth thing. Tonight's the first night."

"Oh, very virtuous!" said Lucy.

Katy smiled in a way she hoped would be perceived as humble. Now that the evening had come around, she'd much rather be two gin and tonics deep at the bar, venting about her boss. What do people talk to teenagers about anyway? Was it too late to cancel? Call in sick?

Her sense of responsibility kicked in. She wasn't one to

let people down at the last moment. She had committed, and she was going to stick to it. And besides, maybe time with a teen stranger was just what she needed. Her work was unfulfilling, her friends were living busy lives, her parents were on yet another cruise, and her outdoor cat hadn't bothered coming home for 24 hours. Maybe it would be nice to feel needed.

At the Community Center, she hung her navy wool coat over her arm and headed to the new volunteers' table, where a friendly lady with enormous reading glasses welcomed her.

"Welcome!" she exclaimed. "I'm Belinda. Is it your first time?"

The large hall pulsed with activity and noise. Fifty kids and fifty tutors were getting connected. It smelled like post-gym class sneakers and drugstore body spray.

"Sorry, what?" She asked over the din.

"First time, right?" repeated Belinda. "Follow me. Let's get you introduced to tonight's student! If you two connect, you can stick with the same student, or if it's not a good match, you will get a new student next week."

Katy's heartbeat quickened, and her stomach lurched. She hadn't realized there would be this element of judgment, that she'd need to get approval, that she'd need to be chosen. It felt like an audition.

Her hope for a match only intensified as Belinda led her through tables of teens. Uncomfortable memories of her high school cafeteria flashed before her, and she wiped her newly sweaty palms on her jeans. It would be much nicer, Katy thought, to have a familiar and friendly face to come back to each week.

At the end of the hall, Belinda stopped before a table with a tutor and two boys.

"Andre, meet Katy. Andre's been with the program since he was ten."

A teenage boy met her eyes. He was balanced on the back two legs of his tilted chair. He had afro hair and a smattering of freckles across the bridge of his nose. He looked up from scrolling on his phone with mild irritation at the interruption and regarded her with minimal interest. He threw a cool nod in her direction, which she returned and threw in a smile. She reminded herself that she was the adult here and not to take it personally.

"The first hour is for homework, and then feel free to grab a game from the game closet for the last 30 minutes. I'll let you get acquainted!" Belinda turned on her heel, her skirt flaring out as she left them.

"Nice to meet you, Andre!" Katy said, hoping she had struck the right balance between enthusiastic and sincere. "What grade are you in?"

"Ninth."

The boy next to him said something under his breath that Katy didn't catch. It must have been funny as Andre started laughing. Katy squirmed and thought of the times she had heard, "It's rude to whisper," as a kid.

"Ah! High school! So, what homework do you have?" She tried again. She had tried for cheery, but it sounded fake, like a talk show host. She wouldn't want to hang out with her.

"I don't have any homework tonight," Andre said, all business.

"Oh," Katy felt a spark of panic. This was already hard work. How was she supposed to entertain this kid for the next hour until game time?

The other boy's tutor noticed Katy's expression and volunteered, "When they don't have homework, you can do this week's essay question." He pointed at a chalkboard back at the other end of the hall with his ballpoint pen like he'd been doing this for years.

A grateful Katy and resigned Andre headed off in silence to read the board. She noted Andre's fashionable clothes and swagger, the ripped jeans and Michael Jordan logos. Diamond-like studs in his ears. Were they real? They were so big.

The girls nudged their friends, preened, and cast coquettish grins as he walked by. A reciprocated smile was met with delighted giggles. The boys called his name, bowing their heads in a respectful nod of acknowledgement. Andre fist-bumped a boy en passant who sat taller after. It was clear; Andre was popular.

She hadn't been a cool kid in high school, and she wasn't a cool adult. Did she need to be cool to relate to him? What did cool people even do? What does a cool kid need?

They stood side by side in front of the board. "Write about a time when you faced adversity in your life," Katy read.

She looked sideways at Andre. He was just a kid, the same height as her. How much adversity could he have faced?

"Got it," he said, turning on his heel.

Back at their table, he put his head down and started to write. He didn't look up to involve her, so she sat by his side and tried not to look like a spare part. His pen moved over the page, his face a picture of earnest concentration. The teenage attitude melted from his features. After a few minutes, curiosity got the better of her and she took a peek over his shoulder.

He hadn't got very far, just a few lines. His penmanship was that of a much younger child, and his spelling was, well, creative. She skimmed over the words *my mother left* and *my best friend gunned down* and *brother arrested,* jumped out at her.

She tried to read the next part, but he glanced at her at that moment. There was no recrimination in his expression, but she felt caught red-handed and averted her eyes as though she had walked in on him changing. He continued writing.

"Let me know if you want help with spelling or anything," she offered.

"OK," he said, not looking up.

While he focused on the essay, Katy stole a closer look at him. The trendy sweater was frayed at the cuff, and his pants had lost some ground to a growth spurt. Bags under his eyes betrayed his fatigue. The toughness was all front.

She felt a flood of compassion for this child, but she was out of her depth. She had lost a grandparent a couple of years ago. A few years before that, she had been heartbroken by the end of a relationship. She had been turned down for jobs. All fairly normal rites of passage. But nothing in her life compared to this kid's experiences.

The hour was up before Andre finished his essay. Katy had provided no value so far. This wasn't going as she imagined. They weren't bonding, and she couldn't blame him. She felt useless. Helping was harder than she'd expected. With 30 minutes to go, there was still hope they could be a match. She needed to connect with something positive. Walking to the game closet, she tried again.

"Weather's getting better, warming up a bit."

"That's when the shooting starts in my neighborhood," he said, stone-faced, not a hitch in his swagger.

Oh jeez.

"What do you do anyway?" he asked.

She appreciated his effort.

"I work in marketing. We provide tools to better automate sales emails."

"Like spam?" he asked.

She conceded that it was like spam.

They walked the rest of the way to the game closet in silence. Partnering again the following week seemed highly unlikely. Katy felt a heaviness in her chest.

They chose *Sorry!* and on the way back to their table to play, Andre got hiccups. He slid her a look. He was embarrassed. She shot back a sympathetic one in solidarity. She sensed his vulnerability. It was hard for him to maintain his cool demeanor while hiccuping, one of the most annoying universal human conditions. Katy sensed an in. Seizing the moment and working off pure impulse, she tried something she had seen work once before.

"I bet you $20 I can cure your hiccups," she said.

He swung around to face her, all skepticism. His full attention was on her now.

"What?" he asked. And hiccuped.

"Your hiccups," she said. "I bet you 20 bucks I can make them stop."

He pantomimed a double take, which made her laugh.

"For real?" A curl formed at the corner of his mouth. He was eager to take her up on the bet.

Her second thoughts were immediate. What was she doing? She realized, of course, he thought she was an idiot, but he was engaging with her at last. She was confident that the first rule of being a tutor was not to gamble with the students. She didn't have $20 if he won, and she certainly wasn't going to take money from him. But the pull of this new connection was too irresistible, and she wanted to see where it would go.

He hiccuped.

"Yes, for real," she said.

They held vivid eye contact. The wager hung in the air that crackled between them. Neither dared to breathe.

His grin grew wider with every second that passed since the last hiccup. Expressions passed like clouds over his face: confidence, incredulity, anticipation, confusion. She had to work to keep her face straight, managing through doubt, amusement, and delight.

And then, it happened. Or rather, it didn't happen. No hiccup came. He stepped back and considered her with bemused interest. This was something new, something he hadn't seen before. It was like a magic trick.

"What? That is crazy!"

It was the first time she saw him smile a real smile. He looked much younger. She was as surprised as he was that it worked, but she played it off like she knew it would. She focused on her poker face, but peppered it with a few meaningful looks, like there was plenty more intriguing stuff that she knew if he just chose to stick around.

Most of all, she felt a new understanding had passed between them. In the quiet space between words and performative coolness, a small but genuine seed of a bond had formed.

"Obviously, you don't need to pay me the money," she said.

"Seriously, how did you do that?" he asked, side-eyeing her.

Katy shrugged; she was still playing it cool as she set up the board, but this cool was different. He was in on it.

"Yo, did you see that?" Andre called to his friend. "That was fire."

Katy allowed herself a small smile.

"Are you coming back next week?" he asked.

"Yes," she said, putting the little pieces in their homes.

"Are you going to be my tutor again?"

"I'd like to," she said truthfully.

"Cool," he said, holding her gaze for just a moment.

Katy smiled and passed him the dice, "You can start."

THE BIG SPOON

"COOKIES, MAMA!" my daughter, Bobbie, yelled. She lurched past me and her Grandma, curls flying, arm outstretched towards a box with a picture of a huge chocolate-studded cookie on it.

"No, sweetie, you've eaten enough junk today already," I sighed.

That morning, Bobbie and I had left home in a hurry, as soon as *he* went to work. For weeks, I had been packing—an item he wouldn't miss here, a few dollars kept from change there. We stopped for breakfast and lunch at fast-food places on the side of the road on the seven-hour drive to my mom's house. Visions of grease-stained napkins, grey meat, and syrup-sticky hands returned like mental indigestion. I already felt like a bad enough parent. I pushed the cart forward.

Bobbie's big brown eyes brimmed with tears, and her lower lip trembled.

"Oh, one little box of cookies won't hurt," my mom said. She ducked behind me and put the box in the cart.

80s hits and the smell of fresh bread filled the store.

George Michael implored us to wake him up before we go-go. I maneuvered the cart so another shopper could navigate around us and caught the metal on my shin. The peppy saxophone screamed, passionate suddenly, in my ears.

I snatched the box from the cart and shoved it back onto the shelf. "I said no!"

"We'll make cookies at home then," Mom said. She smoothed Bobbie's hair, and Bobbie calmed right down as though her soul had been soothed. "Grandma will make you lots of cookies!"

I felt the stretch in my eyebrows and had to look away. Baking cookies? That was a new one. In the spirit of picking your battles, I chose to drop it. It had taken a lot to come back here. I just had to get Bobbie and me back on our feet, and we could move on.

***

The day I left home at 18, just a few days after graduation from my high school, was the last time I saw my mom until today.

"You're making a mistake," she called after me as I got in his black Dodge Charger with my duffel bag. His car had the volatile smell of gasoline and freedom, and the worn leather seats seemed so grown-up. She ran towards the car, and I heard her even over the screeching tires, "This is your home!".

He turned to me and, with a grin full of teeth and a hand on my thigh, he put his foot on the accelerator.

***

The checkout girl's maximalist acrylic nails caught the light as she scanned the barcodes on our food in fluid swipes. She chewed gum as she took us in. "Strong genes in your family. Y'all could be clones."

Mom beamed and looked at me. I rolled my eyes, irritated at what I knew was true. I looked exactly like my mother. The last person I wanted to be like. I bagged up the groceries as Mom fished in her purse for coupons. I scraped up the last of my cash and gave it to her, but she wouldn't take it.

"Keep it," she said. "My treat. It's good to have you back."

I hated that I owed her. I hated that I needed her. I hated that she was being kind.

"Yeah, well, we won't be staying long."

***

Mom was a senior in high school when she had me. Thrown out of her house by her religious parents, she found work as a cleaner. We lived in a trailer to start, shared a bed, and our meals came to us courtesy of the Open Hands Pantry provided by the good people at the Grace United Methodist Church.

At night, in bed, Mom would wrap herself around me, a protective layer that hemmed me in when I needed to stretch. My body curled inward on itself, warmed by her, at times overheated by her, our skin sticky and clammy. On the days she had to rise early for work, my back felt cool and raw with the absence of her, as though I was unfinished and exposed.

She took me to work on days I didn't have school. Left alone to wander other people's houses, I learned quickly that life didn't have to be the struggle it was for us. Mrs Sutton had done it right. Mrs Sutton had married a successful man and had three daughters, each with their own room.

Monroe Sutton was my age. Her room was a fancy of pinks and frills, a mansion dollhouse, and porcelain dolls on her bed. I had no interest in the toys; I would sit at her dressing table and try to force my hair straight with a mother-of-pearl comb. Monroe had balms of rose and lavender that I smoothed on my skin, anointing myself like a cleansing ritual. Then I would lie on the cool of her bedsheets amongst the dolls and, eyes closed, breathe in the scent. It smelled like fresh cotton and safety.

Sometimes I tried on her dresses. She was bigger than me, so when I looked in the dressing table mirror, standing there in those loose clothes, I had to stand on tiptoes and squint a bit to imagine myself in her life.

It wouldn't be the last time I wore those dresses. Mrs Sutton often gave my mother clothes her daughters had outgrown for me to wear. Out of the context of Monroe's bedroom, the outfits lost their mystique and took on a clownish quality. Those wrong-color, out-of-style clothes—I might as well have hung a sign around my neck, 'We're so poor!'

***

When Bobbie and I first pulled up outside Mom's house after the seven-hour drive, I sat in the car and cried. It was as much from the frustration of being back as the relief of getting away. I worked so hard for so long to get away, to make everything different, and yet, here I was, back where I started.

The small brick house looked mostly the same. The grass was a week past due for cutting in the front yard, but flowers bloomed in neat planters on either side of the freshly painted front door. Some garish sun-faded plastic pumpkins I recognized lined the path to the front door. Mom put them out every year. They used to mark the promise of the fun of Halloween, but now, in their weather-worn state, they spoke of relentless repeating cycles.

Mom hesitated on the threshold of the screen door before she came out to the car. I wiped my face on my sleeve.

"Thanks for letting us crash with you."

"Of course, honey. You know you are welcome any time. When you called and said you were coming, well...I was so worried. Let me look at you."

She took my hand, and I cringed away. I couldn't look at her as she searched my face. I wasn't ready for that conversation.

"And is this Miss Bobbie?" Mom cooed, already opening the back door and reaching for Bobbie. Bobbie reached for her, too. They had never met, yet the pull seemed magnetic. "She's your mini-me!"

We shared a common enemy in the carseat straps, which she wrestled with, her urgent thumbs working the latch.

"The buckle thing won't release!"

She tried to bypass the latch and slide Bobbie out. That didn't work.

"Is there a trick to this thing?"

"Want me to do it?" I offered.

She couldn't hear me; she was intent.

Mom broke a nail in the struggle, but at last Bobbie was freed. She held Bobbie to her. Tight, but so gentle, as though she was grafting her to her. She inhaled her. Had Mom held me that way? I guessed she had. I didn't remember it. Did I let her?

***

It started raining as we left the grocery store to drive back to Mom's. Bobbie had fallen asleep in her car seat, rosy-cheeked, thumb in her mouth. "You know I'll pay you back for groceries when I get a job," I said.

"I know love, don't worry about that for now. You're welcome to stay as long as you like, and I can't wait to get to know this little lady." She flicked her eyes up to the rearview mirror to look at Bobbie.

It seemed like Mom was going to keep talking, so I reached out to switch the car radio on, and my sleeve pulled back just enough to reveal bruising around my wrist. I pulled the fabric back down, but Mom had seen.

"Have you left him?" She asked.

"Yes," I said.

"Good. He doesn't know where you are, does he?" she said, eyes on the road.

"No. I don't think he'll guess I've come to you."

She chose to ignore the barb that I wouldn't go to her, even when escaping. In truth, it wouldn't be the first place he'd look, but we both knew that he would come eventually. Bobbie and I would be gone by then.

We rode the rest of the way to her house in silence.
***

On the hot day in summer, I left Mom's house with him all those years ago, I felt life and opportunity stretching out in front of me like the road ahead. I was doing it the right way. He had a good job in sales. He worked hard. I could get a job too, maybe I'd go to college. It would be hard in the beginning, sure, but then we'd make it.

I wouldn't be like my mother. Our children, when they came, would be comfortable. Heck, maybe we'd have a cleaner of our own.

He knew how much I wanted to get away from there, from my life, from her. He whispered, his words like warm treacle, that it was just him and me now.

It was harder than I imagined to find a job in the small town we moved to, but I did find work in a diner. Early starts, blisters on my heels, grill burns on my arms, angry customers —that type of gig. Despite all that, I had grown to enjoy my time at the diner. I became friendly with some of the other girls working there, and I was happy to be making my own, albeit meager, money for once.

By Thanksgiving that year, I was pregnant, and, after a scare with some bleeding, he insisted I quit the job he had been asking me to leave for a while. He had put his hands on my shoulders, his thumbs firm on my collarbones. It wasn't good for the baby for me to be on my feet all day, he reasoned. Things would be tight, but his job was going well enough to support us. I'd stay home, he'd manage the money. We'd make it through.

It was too early to be a mom, too much like my mom. But I had a partner. We had money. My child wouldn't be raised like I was. My child would have two parents. This would be different.

After Bobbie was born, he said it didn't make sense for me to go back to school; I should be home with her. I agreed. I wanted a better life for my daughter.

In Mom's driveway, I carefully lifted Bobbie out of her car seat so as not to wake her. "Honey, why don't you both take a nap? You look exhausted. You can take my bed and put her in your room. I'll bring these groceries in."

I wanted to object, but I was so weary I made my way up the stairs with Bobbie in my arms. From the top of the wooden stairs, I saw that Mom had put a couple of pink towels out for us on my old twin bed. I moved them to the dresser, noting the thoughtful gesture, and laid the still-sleeping Bobbie down on top of the sheets of my twin bed. In the gap her little body left, I slipped behind her and wrapped myself around her.

A couple of hours later, I awoke, disoriented, a blanket now laid over us both. Fully dressed and with a stale taste in my mouth, I could tell by the fading light and my stomach gnawing that it was around dinner time.

***

Mom had a few boyfriends over the years, not many, and none of them stuck. There was a bearded, Stetson-wearing truck driver who snuck me candy when he stayed overnight. Mom didn't like that when she found out. A traveling businessman, who kept calling her 'baby' and kept an erratic schedule, seemed promising until one day his wife called our house. And then there was the one who, over time, raided our pantry until one night all that was left for my dinner was two packets of ketchup, a jar of dill pickles, and some saltines.

Mom and I ate at Denny's that night. We sat opposite each other in a booth, the light low overhead. I loved that rare evening with her. I didn't understand it. Why didn't the men try harder? She gave up on the whole idea of having a man in her life by the time I was in middle school.

Once she kicked the last one to the curb, she worked all the time. One of her cleaning jobs turned into a caregiver job, which she then parlayed into a job in a hospital. It was a stretch for us to live in this house; we were lucky that a grateful son of one of the folks she cared for acted as a guarantor. It was in a better school district, which meant that I stuck out even more than before with my faded hand-me-downs and worn sneakers.

At first, we kept the heat off as much as we could through winter. Appliances stayed unrepaired, and holidays went undecorated.

Mom was working long hours, so to avoid being home alone, I joined after-school clubs. Best of all were the theater clubs; all that rehearsing would give me company and a place to go for weeks. I was good too, regularly cast as the lead. Of course, Mom never made it to the performances. When there was no show in the works, I sought out kids to hang around with at the mall, outside the 7-11, the park, wherever. The parents of the nice kids didn't want me around their children. Beggars really can't be choosers.

Outside of the theater club, it felt familiar, though, to not be chosen, to be an afterthought. I think that's why he was so irresistible when he came.

***

I slipped out of the bed carefully so as not to wake Bobbie. The smell of a rich stew on the stove drew me to the kitchen. "Hey, love," said Mom as she assembled the ingredients for cookies on the round wooden table. The kitchen was homier than I remembered; piles of junk mail and unopened bills had been replaced by a spice rack and an apron, a plant trailed from a macramé holder, and oven mitts hung from a hook on the wall.

"So you have a recipe for cookies?" I asked.

"Tried and tested!" she replied. And then, catching my expression, she froze, flour in her hands. "You're surprised?"

"Well, I don't remember you being the baking kind."

Her shoulders tensed, and she took a deep breath. "What are you saying?"

" I mean, you were never even really at home." I hadn't meant it to sound quite as accusatory as it came out.

Mom sighed and put the flour on the table. "OK, let's have this conversation."

"What conversation?" I was indignant.

"Come on. The one where you tell me what a terrible mother I was," she said.

A flush warmed my cheeks, and before I knew it, the dam burst. "You were never home enough to be a mother! I was all alone. We had nothing. You couldn't even keep a boyfriend."

She arched an eyebrow at the last bit, but her tone was gentle. "I chose to focus on doing everything I could to provide for you, for us. I worked hard, getting into the nursing program, studying, and working shifts. I didn't want to be away from you. I thought you knew that. I couldn't be in two places at once! " Neither of us moved.

"You never even came to my shows!" I threw in.

She turned, opened a cupboard, and retrieved a worn envelope. Without a word, she handed it to me. Inside were photos of me, from every play I'd been in. There I was in a blue dress for Alice in Wonderland and a frilly dress for Eliza Doolittle, a pig in Animal Farm, and a waifish Juliet.

"I dropped my camera off at school and had your teacher take photos." She said simply. "I wanted to build something for us. I was saving for your college. I mean, I'm still building. I've been saving all this time. You weren't ready to go to college before, but I have money put away. I chose you, even though it was hard, just like you're choosing Bobbie. You both can stay here. You will be safe here."

I stared at her. In one step, she wrapped her arms around me very tightly, and I let her, like she was grafting me to her. She squeezed me, and I squeezed her back.

We stayed like that for some minutes until she spoke again.

"Go get Bobbie, she won't want to miss out on making cookies with her Momma and Grandma." With a curl at her lips, she continued. "I certainly could have kept a boyfriend, and I would have if there had been a single one of them that was good enough to be your Dad."

Twenty minutes later, Bobbie, who'd been an eager and hands-on participant in the baking, was covered in flour and butter. Glistening eggshells sat on the tabletop, and the scent of vanilla hung in the air. I popped a chocolate chip that had escaped Bobbie's attention in my mouth and allowed it to melt slowly, savoring the sweetness.

Mom had put some music on, and she sashayed around the kitchen, singing to Bobbie. Seeing Bobbie and Mom rapt in each other's presence, I felt like I had finished a race I hadn't realized I was running. It was wholesome and a complete departure from my own childhood. This is what I had felt was lacking; this is what I hoped for Bobbie. Seeing them together was healing some part of me.

I knew he would come looking for us at some point. And I knew he would find us here. And I knew that I had the strength to send him away. This would be home for Bobbie and me.

Mom picked up the big metal spoon. She was about to stir the batter, but a smile played on her lips as she crouched next to Bobbie. She held it up, like a hand mirror, to show Bobbie her reflection.

"Who's in the spoon?" she asked.

Bobbie looked puzzled. Then she tinkled out a shiny-eyed laugh, and she grabbed the spoon.

"Me and Grandma!" she cried in delight.

I crouched down between them. We laughed as we held each other for balance and tucked in tight so that all three of us fit in the spoon's concave oval. Three tiny people smiled back at us, more alike than not, and upside down.

It would be a different future than the one I had imagined with trappings of success, but it was safe and stable and full of love. And from here I could build, just as my mom had.

RAW EDGES

WHEN THE DOORBELL RANG, she took a moment to decide whether to answer it. But she knew she would. And when she did, there he was—hidden from the waist up behind a huge bouquet.

With a pang, she recognized his muddy sneakers and scruffy jeans. He thrust the flowers forward. A hodgepodge arrangement: gaudy colors, lilies whose stamens stain wherever they fall, and sea lavender whose scent had her nose wrinkling.

Whatever the disagreement had been about felt trivial compared to feeling raw around the edges.

Unfolding her arms, she sighed and plucked the card from between the blooms.

He held his breath while she read.

Sorry.

"Can I come in?" his voice cracked.

She didn't care that he was going to track mud through the house or that the flowers were an eyesore.

"Yes." Her heart swelled.

He stepped forward, lowering the flowers. They embraced. No more raw edges.

ANDROMEDA

COMTESSE ISADORA VON HOHENFELDT found people too slow to be interesting or too needy to be attractive. It was part of the reason she had never married. The other part was that she was the heiress to a castle on a lake, a vineyard, several notable works of art, and a large fortune, none of which she had any desire to share.

As was her custom after the formal dinner at the Captain's table—an undertaking that was only tolerable to her because the staff were briefed on her preferences for minimal interaction and ministered to them assiduously—she strolled on the *Anastasia's* familiar teak deck. She had taken a glass of champagne as she slipped out during the cheese course, finding the époisses and bries an effective distraction. People do love cheese.

The deck was empty save for the occasional white-jacketed butler delivering room service. They nodded discreetly in her direction and gave her a wide berth. She had a deep sense of security, approaching familial comfort, in the understanding she had cultivated with the staff over the years.

It was a calm night. The only wind came from the motion

of the vessel moving through the Mediterranean like a cool iron over black silk. Soft waves were just audible over the distant grand piano and the hum of chatter from the dining room. She stood at the bow of the boat, wisps of her fine ash blonde hair and the hem of her midnight blue dress catching in the breeze.

A crescent moon hung in the ink sky, and between lilac-lined clouds, she could make out the faint fuzzy smudge of Andromeda. Closing her eyes, she took a sip of champagne and let the bubbles and the smooth taste of golden straw linger before swallowing, savoring the vintage and the perfect moment of calm solitude.

"Howdy, Countess!" greeted Maybelle Sterling, a divorced Mom of two college athletes, President of the Dallas Ladies Golf Club, avid horsewoman, and benefactress to numerous local charities—all information Isadora had learned against her will. The American was loud. The woman the Comtesse had been avoiding for the last three days and two ports pulled up to the railing on her left.

Maybelle was a similar age and height to Isadora, but seemed tauter and shinier somehow. Her hair was beauty pageant big, a mane of blond highlights that fanned out and skimmed her bare shoulders. She wore a cerise sateen dress and several enormous diamonds that sparkled like a thousand eyes. She held her champagne flute out to cheers with Isadora, fuchsia-polished talons curled around the stem.

Isadora pulled her mink stole around her shoulders and stood a little straighter, but obliged the toast.

"Cheers," she said through a thin smile and a curt nod, "and please call me Isadora." She returned her gaze out to sea.

Maybelle continued undeterred. "How are you enjoying the boat?"

"The yacht," Isadora paused to underscore the correction, "is splendid."

"Ain't it just? I saw you on the Portofino Abbey day trip. I was trying to say hi."

Isadora had spent that trip hiding behind ancient pillars and tucking inside classical alcoves to avoid just that. She gave a single nod to show she had heard.

"You rushed off so quickly after dinner. They said I could find you out here."

The staff knew better, but she guessed the other guests were not above using her as bait to save themselves. Isadora took a longer sip from her flute; her peace was ruined. A hot flash of irritation burned through her, and she fanned herself with her envelope clutch. Her calm outward demeanor was thanks to her years in a Swiss finishing school, but there were limits.

Conjuring what she hoped was a warm smile, Isadora said, "You know, there is another Texan here! A gentleman that you simply must meet. Very handsome and charming."

"Oh, I'm not trying to meet a guy," said Maybelle.

"Ralph McCoy, from Houston. He's big in oil, extremely successful I believe—" Isadora leaned in when she said that to emphasize the point "—I last saw him in the library toward the stern."

"Oh, honey," said Maybelle. "I don't need a man's money,"

Well, we have that in common, thought Isadora, before redoubling her efforts.

"If you enjoyed the abbey tour, there is an excursion to Arechi Castle. The last chance to sign up is tonight. If you hurry to the bursar, you might still get a spot."

"Bless your heart," Maybelle's tone was saccharine sweet.

"If I didn't know better, I'd think you were trying to get rid of me."

Isadora knew a Texan "bless your heart" was drenched in sarcasm. Maybe there was more to her than met the eye.

The women turned at a discreet cough behind them. "Good evening, ladies. Do pardon the interruption," said a middle-aged butler with a neat combover. "Comtesse, there is a call for you. I have had it patched through to your suite."

"Thank you," she said to the butler. "Do excuse me, Maybelle."

"Have a wonderful evening, Isadora. I'll see you tomorrow. I'm already on the Arechi Castle excursion. I wouldn't miss the 6th-century Byzantine era architecture and the medieval ceramics."

The butler escorted Isadora back to the Tsarina Suite and held open her door for her.

"There's no call, is there, Percy?"

"No, Comtesse. When I saw you standing with Ms. Sterling, it seemed time to initiate the extraction protocol."

"You did well," said Isadora, laying her mink over the back of a velvet armchair. "This one might be different, though. I'll converse with her at breakfast. Keep an eye out, in case we need another interruption."

"As you wish, Comtesse," Percy took the mink and hung it up in a fluid motion. "Will there be anything else this evening?"

"That's all for tonight, thank you, Percy."

Alone in her cabin, Isadora thought it might be nice to get to know Maybelle—with Percy nearby to intervene, of course.

TO THE MOON!

THE NEED for a team-building activity was undeniable. Finger-pointing and recriminations at the tech startup, Orbytor, were at an all-time high after a couple of rough quarters, and morale was at an all-time low. The permanently baseball-hatted wunderkind CEO, Vikram, called Jenny into his office for one of his brainstorming sessions. She put her long mousey hair up into a messy bun and took notes as he pantomimed golf swings. This was their routine.

"How about a cooking class?" Jenny suggested.

Vikram took a swing. Gazing out into space, following the arc of the imaginary ball, he replied, "No, I don't think so. "

"A scavenger hunt?"

"Boring." He teed up again.

She wondered why this step was necessary in his game of fake golf. "There are still a few days of summer left. How about a day out on a boat?"

He grimaced. "No, that's not it," and took another shot before declaring, "Paintball!"

Jenny frowned. A mental vision flashed before her of

Soo-jin, their five-foot-nothing VP of Engineering, and Les, Head of Sales, who'd recently celebrated his sixtieth birthday, wielding paintball guns. She knew Meghan, Head of Operations, mom of four teenagers, and Marcus, VP of Marketing, a man who knew his cashmere from his merino, would much prefer to be sipping a cocktail from a rooftop winebar than commando crawling through the mud. She winced at the image of them all. It was like a demented Saving Private Ryan.

"Is that a good idea...?" she trailed off.

"Absolutely! RedGenie's new feature set is another total rip-off of ours—"

"We truly are their product development team," sighed Jenny, shaking her head.

"—and, according to LinkedIn this morning, Cynthia ended up as their new Product Manager."

"That snake!" said Jenny. "Well, good luck to them, dealing with her constantly changing priorities and asking for a raise every month."

"Yes, that one is a win for us," Vikram said. "Let's get out there and rediscover our mojo. We've got to get this team back together, or we've had it."

Vikram returned to his swivel chair, grabbed a plush football from his desk, and made as if to launch it across the room. He did this a few times, his sign that the conversation was over. Jenny knew he was right about RedGenie; the threat was real. The Orbytor team was magic when they were in sync, but at the moment, they were falling apart. She thought of her stock options and said a silent prayer.

***

Two weeks later, the budget-friendly van Jenny booked

for the event was idling outside the office. It bore the wear and tear of a thousand youth groups and smelled like damp socks. Jenny, dressed in a pair of leggings and an old college t-shirt she'd been meaning to donate, ushered Soo-jin into the van.

"Late as usual," muttered Les.

"Oh well, pardon me! I was just fixing a mission-critical bug!" snarked Soo-jin.

"When are we leaving?' asked Meghan.

"Any minute, just waiting for Vikram," said Jenny. "Ah, here he comes!"

Jenny was relieved it had only taken three texts, two voice calls, and a calendar invite to get him there. He bounded on board, seeming impervious to the smell, fist-bumped the air, and called out the company cheer, "To the moon!". He high-fived his irritable management team (and the moustachioed driver) on his way to the back of the van, whereupon he spread his long arms wide, taking up the entire row.

Finally underway, Jenny distributed Orbytor merch: navy hoodies emblazoned with the Orbytor logo—a large rocket—and their "To the moon!" slogan. Peering over her reading glasses, Meghan registered that Jenny had also splurged on water bottles. She rolled her eyes and tutted at the additional expense.

Marcus felt the fabric of the hoodie, and Jenny swore she saw him shudder.

At least Soo-jin was pleased. She dressed almost exclu-sively in the freebies she had scored from previous jobs and conferences.

The van sped out of Boston, bouncing along the highway. The further they got from the city, the wider the summer sky seemed to open up. They passed on old farms with peeling white paint on their siding, and hand-drawn signs advertising blueberries and corn.

"Why are we going so far?" complained Soo-jin to Jenny.

"It's such a waste of time going all this way out of town," added Megahn. "We should be cutting costs, not adding them."

"No customer prospects out here!" chimed in Les.

"Why paintballing?" asked Marcus. "It's not exactly an executive-friendly activity."

Jenny knew they'd never ask Vikram these questions. And she knew how to shut them up.

"It was Vikram's idea."

Quiet descended over the group, and they all settled down for the journey. Marcus made good use of the sleep mask he had brought with him. Soo-jin jerryrigged a gaming system, juggling two monitors and wearing headphones that would have been at home on a helicopter pilot. White earphones peeked out under Vikram's baseball cap. Eyes closed, his head nodded, and his knee bounced along to the beat of whatever he was listening to. From time to time, he bit his lower lip and performed a drum solo on an imaginary drum set. Les held his newspaper up, forming a physical barrier with the rest of the team. Meghan, whose children's schedules were stacked with extracurricular activities, worked on forms for the PTA, Girl Scouts, and a cake sale. She fanned herself with the papers.

Jenny sighed. At nearly thirty years old, her friends were deep into meaningful careers. Some were married, and two were pregnant, all while she'd been stuck with this bunch of misfits.

The product at Orbytor was still strong—heck, competitors cloning it —and the team was peerless, especially when they pulled in the same direction, but her career had stalled, and she was sick of the dysfunction. She wanted something with more impact than the miscellaneous admin role she had landed in. She resolved to update her resume. If the team couldn't come together today, it was time to move on.

The van pulled into SPLAAAT!, the paintballing place Jenny had booked. No sooner were the team gathered in the parking lot than a luxury bus pulled in behind them. Out piled half a dozen executives, laughing and chatting. They were attractive, with shiny hair and straight, white teeth. They wore sleek scarlet uniforms emblazoned with the RedGenie logo and 'Your wish, Our command'. The Orbytor team was frozen, suddenly self-conscious.

"Oh great," said Soo-jin.

"What the hell are they doing here?" Marcus whispered to Jenny as if she should know.

"Great minds think alike, I guess," said Vikram.

The RedGenie team's over-the-top enjoyment of themselves seemed to intensify in proportion to Orbytor's discomfort. They moved to the reception area like a slow-motion hair commercial. The men, the women, they were all beautiful.

"Close your mouth, Les," said Marcus.

"Is it me, or is it hot?" asked Meghan.

The Orbytor crew realized the RedGenie team would get to the check-in desk first. It felt like another loss. They watched from wooden benches as RedGenie received their overalls, guns, and masks. Three of their female execs arranged themselves into the Charlie's Angels pose with their paintball guns, flirtatious laughs filling the check-in area. Soo-jin and Jenny exchanged eye rolls. Les seemed to perk up.

"We aren't playing against them, are we?" asked Marcus.

"No, we have a private area separate from them," Jenny reassured him.

"Oh, thank goodness," said Soo-jin.

"We could play against them," said Vikram. He was doing the golf swing thing again.

"I don't think that's a good idea," said Meghan. RedGenie looked downright athletic.

"It's a great idea. I believe in this team. In fact—" Vikram stood up "— we must play them." He strode over to the RedGenie group.

Jenny watched Vikram and the easy way he approached the tallest member in their team. They were already laughing together, all broad smiles. As they shook hands, she realized that they would be playing against RedGenie.

She turned to face the group. "Now don't freak out—"

But it was too late.

"It's game on!" Vikram called from across the check-in room. "To the moon!" He punctuated this with a fist pump.

Ten minutes later, decked out in their paintball gear, the Orbytor team emerged from their cabin into the battle zone. Sunlight through the leaves dappled their fatigues.

Despite Jenny's instructions to wear pants, Meghan had worn a dress, which she had to bunch up to fit under her overalls. The effect was suggestive of a fourth baby, well on the way. She patted her round belly. "Good to have a bit more padding!"

Soo-jin was drowning in her overalls; the smallest size they had was medium. She looked like a child. "Maybe they'll go easy on me?"

"You're such a small target they'll have to be crack shots to hit you," laughed Vikram.

Marcus had popped the collar up on his fatigues. Jenny

knew he'd have a trick up his sleeve to make the bulky outfit more stylish.

Les had found a black strip of fabric and tied it around his head, Rambo style. He pulled the headgear over it. He was in the zone.

Vikram bounced from foot to foot, holding his gun across his body.

They were not an imposing group.

"When does it start?" asked Meghan.

"Er, I think they sound an alarm or something," said Jenny.

"What if I get shot?" asked Les.

Soo-jin shuddered.

"Les, if we have to explain the rules to you one more time, I swear—" said Meghan.

"You have to leave the battle zone and you're out," said Jenny.

"Does it hurt?" asked Soo-jin.

"Yeah, I think it hurts," replied Jenny. No point lying; they would find out for themselves soon enough. "Listen, we've got two games. Let's just get through them."

A whistle pierced the calm of the woods and sent a family of crows flapping from their tree perch.

"Oh god," said Soo-jin. "It's like an omen of doom."

"To the moon!" called Vikram. They looked a sorry sight, trampling single file through the scrub. After a minute, they emerged into a clearing and reformed their circle, awaiting instruction.

Phut phut phut. Bullets whizzed past Jenny before she realized what was going on. And then a sharp sting on her thigh, which bloomed yellow paint and left a hot ache, swiftly followed by another on her shoulder. She'd been hit.

"Ouch!" exclaimed Les, clasping a hand to his left buttock.

In a hail of bullets worthy of a Tarantino film, the rest of the team suffered the same fate and were covered in splodges of yellow paint.

It was a massacre.

Whoops from the RedGenie team, still unseen in the bushes, only served to dampen the Orbytor team's mood further.

"I guess we're all out," said Soo-jin.

"Whose idea was this?" grumbled Marcus.

"Why did we just follow Vikram out into the open like that?" Meghan asked. "Like absolute idiots."

"Why did you follow me? You're all leaders yourselves."

The question hung in the air as the Orbytor team trudged back to their base.

There was no need to reload during the ten-minute break between games. The team hadn't been able to get off a single shot.

"They came at us like the Viet Cong!" wailed Les.

Jenny wrinkled her nose. Was that racist? There were many occasions during her time with Orbytor when she wished they had an HR department.

"Sneaky underhand tricks," said Meghan. It was the first thing Meghan and Les had agreed on for weeks.

"I hate RedGenie," said Marcus, kicking at a pile of leaves. "They copy our product ideas, they steal our customers—"

"They riddle us with bullets," added Les.

"We need a plan this time," said Soo-jin.

"Well, don't look at me!" said Vikram, feeling all eyes on him. "I don't know any more about paintball than you do."

They all turned to Jenny.

"Oh, come on!" she said.

"OK, no going out in a big group again. We need to split up," said Meghan.

"We should go in twos," said Les.

"We've got them this time," said Vikram, hopping from foot to foot.

A whistle signified that the second round had started, and the Orbytor pairs peeled off on different paths into the woods.

"Listen, Jenny," said Les in a hushed tone. "Can we talk frankly? You know, open kimono —"

"Oh my god, Les!"

"I'm just saying, you can be honest with me. You've seemed a bit down recently. Are you OK?"

She shouldered her way past a low branch harder than she needed to. "I'm fine, let's just focus on kicking some RedGenie butt."

"Sounds good to me."

About ten steps further, Les tripped on a log and yelped. A spray of bullets peppered the trees by them.

"I'm hit!" he called out. "I'm down!" The paint splotch was blue. "What the heck? Friendly fire!"

"Sorry!" Meghan's voice came from the thicket fifty feet away. "It was pure instinct!"

"Good grief," said Jenny, who was somehow unscathed. "With friends like this..."

"Jenny, come over with us," called Meghan.

"I'm coming, but be quiet!" hissed Jenny, making a crouched run through the clearing to join Marcus and a sheepish-looking Meghan who were sitting cross-legged on the dirt under a large bush.

"Honest mistake," said Meghan with a shrug.

"What's the plan here?" said Jenny, squatting next to them.

"We're lying in wait," said Marcus. "We chill here, and we just pick them off, one by one."

The trio heard Vikram and Soo-jin before they saw them. Approaching from the left, the pair made short dashes between trees, running with high knees, ducking behind each trunk, only to poke their heads out again to check the coast was clear. They were not discreet.

"They're being stalked!" said Marcus in an urgent whisper. "Enemy combatants at three o'clock!"

Sure enough, to the right, there were two RedGenie players in stealth mode. They placed their feet heel to toe, in controlled movements, to avoid snapping twigs.

"We have to warn them!" said Meghan.

The three of them emerged from the thicket and made frantic pointing motions. Soo-jin and Vikram appeared from behind a tree with confused faces and volleyed back with shrugs. This exchange was cut short by a splinter group from RedGenie who had snuck up behind the trio and shot them at close range. Vikram and Soo-jin met the same fate just moments after that.

Back in the cabin, the mood was dejected. They were all smeared with yellow neon paint. Les had additional blue splotches where Meghan had shot him.

"I got paint in my mouth," said Les.

"I'll get you a mint," said Meghan, reaching into her purse.

"Why did you blow our cover?" Soo-jin asked. "We were fine!"

"We were saving you!" said Marcus.

"Great job, everyone!" said Vikram. "Well done getting out there and giving it a go."

Jenny was quiet. She sat with her head in her hands. She had had it with these people.

"Great job organizing everything today, Jenny," said Vikram as the team walked back through the parking lot to the van. "Thank you for all that you do for this company."

Jenny stared at him in disbelief. "Are you serious right now?"

"Yes, it's been a wonderful day."

"Vikram," she said in as even a tone as she could manage. "The team is miserable. They are more annoyed with each other now than when we started. This was a terrible idea."

"The day's not over yet, Jenny!"

It was a sorry bunch who climbed back into the van.

"You didn't win then?" asked the driver, reading their body language.

The ride back to Boston was subdued.

"Friends of yours?" asked the driver, gesturing to a gleaming luxury bus that had pulled up alongside them.

"Ugh, it's RedGenie," said Soo-jin.

Sure enough, their smug rivals were in the next lane over, stuck in the same traffic. Their faces were contorted into ugly sneers as they laughed and pointed at the Orbytor team. They were flashing victory signs, pumping their fists, and filming them with their phones.

"Stop filming us!" Marcus made a shooing motion with his arm.

"Just ignore them," said Jenny.

"Are they miming a rocket, like in our logo?" asked Les.

"Like it's launching, over and over?" guessed Soo-jin.

"Oh," said Marcus, dismayed. "That's not a rocket."

"Oh, absolutely not," said Meghan, clocking the obscene

gesture, her cheeks tinged pink. "We paid good money for that branding, and I've had just about enough of those assholes and their antics." And with that, the middle-aged mother of four stood up, braced herself against the seat in front of her, hitched up her dress, pulled down her underwear, and pressed her rear against the window of the van. "That's what I think of that!"

"I can't let you go this alone, Meghan," said Les with reverence, already unbuckling his belt.

"What's going on back there?" asked the driver, sensing the commotion.

Soo-jin stood too. And in no time, there was a fleshy representation from three of the Orbytor exec team.

"What. Is. Happening?" said Jenny, mostly to herself.

"They are not better than us!" shouted Soo-jin.

"Damn right," agreed Marcus, finding his own spot against the glass.

"They don't call this the rear view mirror for nothing!" The driver chuckled, pleased with his joke. "Just be careful!"

"To the moon!" cheered Vikram, climbing over the seat to squeeze in between Les and Soo-jin.

The rest of them joined in chanting, "To the moon! To the moon!"

Jenny was motionless. They looked ridiculous. After the way the day had gone, she had decided to hand in her notice after her next paycheck. But the last five years of her career had been with these people. They had been through thick and thin together. And here they were, bruised and battered, their rear ends pressed to a pane of glass on the busiest stretch of the I-93. United at last, albeit in the most Orbytor of ways. She closed her eyes for a moment and took a deep breath.

"You might be idiots," she said, and added with a smile. "But you're my idiots."

A new buzz went through the group as they cheered and clapped, scooching over to make a spot for her in the middle. The window was cool and grounding on her skin. To her left and right, her teammates chanted and grinned at each other. She loved these fools.

Traffic started moving in their lane, the van jerked forward, and they all grabbed each other for support. As they pulled ahead of RedGenie, other commuters saw what was happening, and the highway broke out into a cacophony of car horns.

For the next week, footage of the 'exhibition' did the rounds on social media. Each time it circulated, Marcus was sure to add the hashtags #tothemoon #orbytor. Within a couple of weeks, they were all over HackerNews, TechCrunch had done a write-up about them, investors were lining up, and their sales pipeline had quadrupled in size.

Vikram called Jenny into his office, where she found him back at the invisible driving range.

"Our star is on the rise again, Jenny," he said. "A lot of it thanks to a successful day at paintball. Thanks again for organizing it."

Jenny laughed. "We lost at paintball. Everyone was fed up. It was a mess."

"Exactly!" said Vikram with an enigmatic smile. "I'm going to need back-up for what's next. How would you like to be my Chief of Staff?"

ACKNOWLEDGMENTS

Thanks to Tom Beeckman, Sonesh Chainani, Julie Connors, Jeffrey and Ricki Dorn, Suzi Edwards-Alexander, Amy Naim, Joss Norton, Helen Preston, C. V. Shaw, South Florida Writers Association, Cynthia Uzzolino, and Tess Zelechowski for support, encouragement, and thoughtful feedback. The stories collected here are better for having been polished by their insight; all remaining rough edges are entirely my own.

Special thanks to Dr. Louise Savic, who gave medical expertise and hours of encouragement.

Thanks to my parents, for my fabulous hair and my sense of humor—two gifts that have served me well.

Thanks to the best siblings a girl could have: James Avent and Lucy Gabb—your love and infectious enthusiasm mean everything.

Thanks to Daisy, who is a very good girl, and is the inspiration for both Goat and Mitzy.

Thanks to my children, Millie and Sam, who let me read to them when they were little and now serve as thoughtful, wise, and mostly diplomatic beta readers. You make me proud every day.

And to my husband, Matt—without whom I would have two fewer beta readers and far less laughter. Thank you for your relentless love and support, your high tolerance for whatever shiny object I'm chasing, and your strong punctuation skills.

Finally, to you, dear reader—thank you for taking a chance on these stories and spending your time in their company.

ABOUT THE AUTHOR

Jo Avent's poem Friendly Moon appears in The Sea of Tranquility Anthology and is scheduled to be shot into space in December 2025 as part of the Lunar Codex project. This is her first collection of short stories.

Jo grew up in the UK, and lived in France and Spain before moving to the United States. After toughing out well over a decade of Chicago winters, she now lives in Miami with her husband, their two children, and their retired dog.

When she isn't writing she can be found making wonky pots, enjoying coffee and chats with friends, and attempting various yoga poses.

Jo is fascinated by people; what makes them tick, and the choices they make.

You can find her sharing updates on instagram. She loves to hear from her readers.

 instagram.com/joiswriting